888 796 82~

Crisis

walk in

333 North Br~

ave

TRAP LAND

workpartners

1800 6331/97

3 to 5 days

will call

Lead

Nicholas

TRAP LAND

by

Anthony Boykin

Acknowledgments

First I would like to thank my Lord and Savior Jesus Christ. I will continue to give you my praise and devotion, my soul is yours Lord and yours only.

Next I want to thank my wife and children April L Lee Boykin, William J Lewis, Shantell L Boykin and Abrea T Boykin y'all are the reason I push to be great.

I want to thank my partner Gina Camp and her husband for helping me achieve the beginning of my dream of becoming one of Pittsburgh's best authors. I look forward to work with you guys.

I want to thank my big cousin IkeWear CEO Donny Kyte, without you pushing me to finish, this book would still be in my drawer at work. I wish for nothing but great things for you cuz.

Now I'm going to give a few shout outs to some of the people that I got love for. Marrell Childs, Nona Lee, Bonnie Cobbs, Gerald Lee, Wayne Boykin, Kenny Boykin, Danielle Kyte, Marty Child's, Tia Childs, Danny Kyte, Darnell West, Latasha Kyte, David Monroe Jr, Lori Coleman, Robin Gray, Shawnesha Johnson, Raymar McCombs and all my nieces and nephews. Free Andre Jackson & Tarrell Childs I ant forget y'all.

Last but not least I want to thank you the reader for buying and supporting me as an author. I look forward to entertaining you with different styles of exciting books for you to read for years to come.

Chapter 1

It was a cold winter night in the mean streets of Pittsburgh City. Police sirens blended with the sounds of the leafless branches swaying as the cold winter wind blew. A section of the court was taped off while two lifeless bodies laid on the cold pavement. The police were at the scene investigating the double homicide, which made the death toll that year rise to seventy-three.

The crime had been witnessed by a set of twelve year old twins who happened to be up late that night. In shock of what they saw, they vowed to never speak a word to anyone about it. The detectives knocked on every door in the court trying to find someone who might have seen what had happened. They briefly questioned thirteen families that lived in the court. They quickly became aggravated, coming up short on any information that could lead to a possible suspect or arrest. They had absolutely nothing to go on.

Detective Bill Gray knew this wasn't going to be an open and shut case due to the fact that snitching was like a death sentence in this neighborhood. If you got caught talking to the police, it was on! But, Detective Gray was going to make sure he spent most of his time on the Hill District, hoping he will stumble across a lead.

$

"Yo Ike, I'm tired of taking these old motherfucker's garbage out! We got to find a new way to get this money bro," Jason whined to Jermaine while throwing the hefty bag in the dumpster. Jermain nodded in agreement, still a little in shock about what happened the night before. The two were twins whose mother smoked more crack than ten fiends put together. Their dad couldn't put up with her drug use, so he split, leaving the boys to fend for themselves.

Over the years, the twins would make store runs for the niggas that hustled in their court. The boys grew close to a few of them, but the nigga Gold would be the one who takes the boys under his wing.

"Gold what's up my nigga?" O.G. Blood spoke to Gold as he walked in the hallway.

"Slow as fuck my nigga. But what's up with you?"

"Same shit... Yo, dickhead Gray is posted in front of Roxy's court."

While O.G. Blood was talking, Gold was rolling a blunt of purple and bubble gum Kush, putting his famous twist on it as he finished. Before standing, he brushed the weed particles off his lap, showing no emotion, yet a little nervous about what he did last night. As many thoughts ran through his mind, he was sure no one in that court would rat on him, but he wasn't sure what evidence the D's was able to scramble up. Shit, the shells were clean and the gun was at the bottom of the Ohio River and that thought eased his mind a little.

He replied to O.G. Blood, "So the dickhead ass jakes are in Roxy's court? Shit, I did them faggot ass mother fuckers a favor by killing them New York niggas, you know Ike?"

"I know bro," O.G. Blood replied back as Gold passed him the blunt.

$

"Hide over here!" Jason said to Shameka while playing hide and go seek. He led her to a vacant hallway in one of the courts behind his. Shameka laughed while ignoring his hand on her ass. He has been trying to get in her panties for a minute now, coming up short every time, but today he was in for a surprise.

He kissed her neck and her body shivered as she stood there motionless, feeling the sensation of her virgin pussy becoming wet. She wanted him more than ever now, but was scared of him penetrating her since she'd never done it before. As Jason's hands rubbed on her ass, she remembered hearing some of the other girls talk about keeping their man satisfied by giving him some good head.

"Jason, I want our first time to be special."

As she began to talk, Jason thought to himself, "Here we go again!" He wasn't ready for what was about to happen.

Shameka sat on the last step and reached for the shoe string that served as Jason's belt. She positioned her face in front of his crotch and reached up to pull his dick out. She slowly began taking him in and out of her mouth, twirling her tongue around the head. Only a few minutes in and they were interrupted by a bang on the hallway door. Jason hurried to pull his pants up as Shameka wiped her mouth and stood up abruptly.

"I know yall in there!" A voice screamed through the crack of the door. "Let me in Ike!"

It was Jermaine, ditching a little fat girl that was chasing him. Jason and Shameka decided to finish at another time. Jason have grown use to Jermaine cock-blocking, which was his title between the two.

Chapter 2

Later on that night around 7:30, Gold was trappin' in the twin's hall. He knew the twins saw him kill them two niggas last night and figured he would have a talk with the boys soon. He had become like an older brother to them, buying them sneaks and Play Station games whenever they came through the hood hot and shit.

After serving the last fiend, Gold lit his ninth blunt of the day. When the hallway door flew open, the twins walked in the hall. Jermaine, a little nervous at the sight of Gold, put his head down avoiding eye contact. Jason on the other hand had no fear and thought what Gold did was some straight gangster shit.

"What's up with my young niggas?" Gold said to the boys while reaching to give them some daps. "Yall hungry?" He asked.

"Hell yeah!" Jason replied while dapping' Gold up.

"That's what's up... I got some Pizza Hut already on the way. Jermaine what's wrong? You look like you just seen a ghost," Gold said while grabbing him in a headlock.

Gold wrestling and joking with Jermaine made him feel a lot better. He was no longer looking in the eyes of a killer. He was looking in the eyes of the only older nigga that gave a fuck about the two.

"So yawl was up pretty late last night hmm?" Gold asked the boys while playfully punching Jason in the hallway.

"Yeah, me and Jermaine were playing Mortal Kombat and then we heard all these gun shots."

While Jason was telling Gold the story, Jermaine went to go let the pizza man in. After the pizza man left out, Jermaine looked at Gold and asked, "Why?" Gold knew what he was talking about but didn't really know how to respond.

Those two New York niggas had raped the twins' mom. A couple of days earlier, Roxy let them lame ass niggas cook their coke in her house. After finishing, the nigga Seven convinced Roxy to give him some head and she agreed, but when she refused to suck his man's dick, he punched her in the face and they both took turns ramming their dicks in and out of every hole you could imagine. Coming pass to see the boys, Gold found Roxy beaten and raped on her living room floor. She explained to Gold what happened and he took it from there. Three days later, Gold's crazy ass seen the two niggas and visions of a raped and beaten Roxy entered his head. Gold pulled a Point 40 from his waist and fired shots at the two of them, hitting both before running off.

Gold wanted to tell the boys what happened, but thought it was Roxy's place to do that so he just told them that the niggas got what they deserved. He further explained to them about disrespect and how to handle it.

The three sat and ate pizza while Gold schooled the boys on some of the shit he go through while trying to get that money. After eating like four pieces, Jermaine went in the house and was sleep by the time Jason came in. While still in the hallway, Jason tried to talk Gold into helping him put his foot in the game.

A few years later, Gold ended up doing more than put the youngin's foot in the game – he brought him straight to the top.

Chapter 3

"Yo, I need you to go meet these niggas out Homewood for me. They got some new shit that's supposed to be fire."

"So what's in it for me?" Jason asked.

"A black eye if you don't hurry your ass over there." Gold replied to Jason, who was now seventeen and running as Gold's right hand man.

Jason jumped in his 1989 Regal and made it burn rubber as he pulled away from the court. Gold and Jason became the top dogs over the last three years and were supplying half of the Hill.

Jason was headed east on Fifth Ave with Jay Z's "Hard Knock Life" banging through the twelve inch woofers. He had to meet a nigga named Burner at the YMCA on Brushton Ave and was a bit nervous considering he was about to ride through one of the hardest Crip neighborhoods in the Burgh. After taking a pull from the blunt of purple, he calmed himself down and made the left onto Homewood Ave, and then another onto Brushton. Gold told him that Burner would be in the parking lot in a black CTS. As he pulled into the lot, he noticed Burner's car parked but still running. As Burner noticed Jason's car pulling into the parking lot he began to slowly pull out of the parking spot he was in. Both cars pulled beside each other as Jason's window came down. Burner threw a brown paper bag through Jason's window and without any words, both cars pulled off.

{"It's a hard knock life for us... It's a hard knock life for us...Instead of kisses, we get kicked"}

While listening to one of Jay Z's hit songs, Jason sang along with the hook, thinking of the hard knock life he and his brother lived as kids. After riding for a minute he noticed a police car about a car length behind him, so he turned his music down as he approached the red light. When the light turned green, he made the left onto Millville. Once he noticed the police car continue to go straight he turned his sounds back up. "A few blocks more," he thought to himself. Jason was a deep thinker and for the rest of the ride his thoughts wondered like crazy.

$

"Where's my money nigga, don't make me put this hot shit in yo! It was only a whole one Ike – you aren't done yet?"

"Damn Gold, you know I got you my nigga! Have I ever played you Ike? I'll bring it to you tomorrow for sure my nigga. But what's up with some new shit? This shit ain't moving like that Ike."

Paul explained to Gold how the fiends been complaining. It was a drought in the city and everybody was stretching their coke to the maximum limit, but Gold was about to change that.

As Paul walked out of the hallway, he noticed the crowd of fiends in front of the hallway where he be trappin' out of. He overheard one of them talking shit about how nasty his coke was as he jogged over to make the sales. While making the snaps, he was ready to put it on Jack for talking shit on his product, but the hundred and fifty dollars All-night had eased his anger. He only needed like three hundred dollars to make his quota for the day and to his surprise he was able to make the whole $300 off this one rush. So he headed back to pay Gold to make sure he was one of the one's to get some of the new shit.

$

After parking, Jason grabbed the bag of coke and got out the car. While opening the hallway door, he heard Gold and someone else talking. As he walked up the steps, he noticed that Gold was talking to Pimpin' Paul. Jason really didn't like most of the older niggas Gold fucked with. They were downfalls in his mind – All they did was beg. "Gold front me this, Gold, front me that," a bunch of washed up hustlers looking for their next handout.

"Gold, we got business," Jason stated while cutting Gold's conversation short.

Gold dapped Paul up and told him he would call him later. While walking up the steps, Gold let Jason think he was running shit as part of lesson one: Always take charge of the situation and never delay important business.

$

Ms. Ross had everything set up for them. She had the pot of water boiling on the stove and the napkins and scale set on the table. As soon as they went in, they went straight to work. Gold poured the coke in the Pyrex, then put the Pyrex into the pot of hot water. Within minutes, the coke started to melt. As it was melting, he put fifteen grams of baking soda into the melting two and a half ounces of coke and then sprinkled a tea spoon of hot water into the Pyrex. After stirring the shit up, he took the Pyrex out the pot of hot water and put it in a bowl of ice water. In a matter of minutes, it was rock hard.

"Bai-yow," Jason said after tapping the coke with a butter knife. "That shit hard as hell Ike!"

With no response to Jason's excitement, Gold put the Pyrex back in the pot for about another minute. After taking it out, he tapped the top of the Pyrex on the table and "Clunk" was the sound it made as the coke fell out.

"This shit look like fire Ike," Gold said as he put the coke on the scale. Seventy eight grams is what it read.

"Only eight grams extra," Jason said in an uncertain tone.

"That's what we want, that melt nigga. We're going to take over with this shit here," Gold replied as he broke a little piece off. "Yo, go give Ms. Ross this. See how she likes it." He handed Jason the piece he broke off for her to test.

"Ms. Ross, tell me what this is like," Jason stated as he walked in her room. Ms. Ross threw the piece in her chumpy and after one pull, her eyes rolled into the back of her head and her jaws clinched as she enjoyed a high she haven't felt in years.

"Damn Boy, this is that Tony the Tiger shit, it's Grrreat," she responded while putting her pipe back on the table.

"So it's good?"

"Yeah, that shit is bomb," she replied as Jason walked out of the room.

"Hello," Jason said, answering his phone. "What up nigga?" A female's voice echoed through. "Handling some business," he replied. "Well we got business tonight right?" "Oh, fa sure, I'mma call you soon as I finish up with Gold."

On the other end of the call was Shameka who was now Jason's main squeeze. And being that she had a head on her shoulders, Gold would encourage Jason to do right by her.

"Yo, who was that," Gold asked as Jason waked back into the kitchen.

"Shameka," Jason replied as Gold threw him a bag of coke. He caught it on instinct. "What's this Gold?"

"Seventy grams, it's yours bro. I'mma call you once I get back in touch with these niggas."

"Ok my nigga. I'll see you later, One," Jason replied as he walked out the door.

$

"Shamekaaaa!" Ms. Bell yelled as she opened the door, seeing it was Jason.

"Hi you doing Ms. Goddess maker," Jason joked with Ms. Bell while walking into the living room. "Fine Jason, and you?"

"I'm ok. A little tired, but ok."

"Hey baby," Shameka said as she walked into the living room. "Mom, what time are you leaving?"

"When my ride get here Ms. Missy. Why you"...

"Ms. Bell, would you like to use my car," Jason asked before Ms. Bell could shoot a nasty remark at Shameka.

"Sure baby, Thanks," she replied while cutting an evil eye at her daughter.

"No problem Ms. Bell. When my money get right, I'mma put you in a nice whip. Something tight."

"That's nice of you to say Jason, now I will see yawl later.

After Ms. Bell left, Jason and Shameka went into her bedroom. Jason laid on the bed while Shameka rolled a blunt. They got high and fell asleep — after about a half hour of hard sex.

The next day, Jason was awakened by the sound of his cell phone.

"Hello! You this" Jason asked as he answered the call.

"What up my nigga, it's Larry?" The voice on the other end echoed through.

"Just getting up my nigga."

"Well get the fuck up! I got like twenty-two hundred for you right now nigga!" Lil Larry stated as he made the left onto Center Ave.

"Oh yeah! Let me call you back in like a half hour... Matter of fact, meet me at my mom's in a half." Jason replied.

"My niggaaaa, I'll be there."

$

"Man, could we go to the mall before you get too busy bay," Yalonda asked while walking back in the room. Gold gave no answer as he looked through his phone for the number to the Crip niggas that had the new shit.

"Baby!" She cried in a sexy voice, hoping to get a positive response as she laid her head on his lap and unbutton the crouch button of the night pants

"Yeah Baby, we can go to the mall. Just let me handle this and we out."

"Thank you Baby," she said while slipping him into her mouth, trying to give him a quick shot of head.

"I said yeah Ma, Damn!" Gold spoke in a frustrated tone.

He couldn't remember what number he put those niggas under. Instead of names, he would use numbers so that if he ever got pinched, the police wouldn't be able to get nobody's name out of his shit.

"Bai-yow!" He said to himself as he came across the numbers 456. He sang to himself, "456 Tioga Street Crip."

"Aye, go get dressed and we out," Gold said as he moved her head out of his crotch. Now in a better mood, he made the call while Yalonda got in the shower.

"Yo, what up nigga?" It's Gold speaking numbers."

"Pep Boys, 3:30," the voice on the other end of the phone stated before hanging up.

Gold was trying to buy three keys and wasn't trying to pay more than fifty-eight thousand. That was less than twenty a piece and the price in the hood was twenty-three and that was on a good day. After doing the math, he would save eleven grand. He thought it was worth a try.

"Yalonda! Hurry your ass up!" Gold yelled

"I'm coming baby." She replied, thinking about what Jimmy Choo's she was going to get to rock with the Club Monaco dress she had bought in Vegas. She was always trying to shit on the other bitches. She was always fly though.

$

After getting to his mom's, Jason scrambled through the kitchen drawers looking for his scale.

"Mom! ... Mom!" Jason screamed.

"What boy?" Roxy screamed back.

"Did you see my scale?"

"It's on top of the refrigerator."

After finding the skee-wop, he broke two ounces off the seventy grams Gold gave him and then called Lil Larry.

"Where you at?" Jason said into the phone.

"About to pull up!"

"Alright, I'm in my mom's."

A few minutes later, Larry was walking through Roxy's door. Jason gave Larry the two ounces and told him that the price would go down on the next flip.

Jason had a little crew he ran with and Lil Larry was Jason's right hand man. Jason and Lil Larry got cool a couple years ago. Lil Larry helped Jermaine and Jason crush these niggas one day at a party. Jermaine was the only one that got caught and was charged with aggravated assault and sentenced to two years in a juvenile detention center up in Erie for nearly killing one of the niggas. While in locked up, Jermaine beat up one of the staff members and got an extra six months. He's due to come home in three months, as long as he doesn't get in any more trouble while he's there. Until then, Lil Larry would serve as Jason's right hand man, handling the hand-to-hand sales in the hood as Jason took care of the big business.

Lil Larry had a nice hustle game and was dedicated to putting mad hours in on the block. Jason admired Lil Larry's work ethic because he hated to sale to the fiends. Larry would stay on the block for days making thousands serving nothing but the fiends.

$

It was like 11:30 a.m. when Gold and Yalonda arrived at the mall. Yalonda's sexy ass wanted to stop in Victoria's Secret first, knowing that this was the only store Gold didn't mind helping her shop in. He loved to help her pick out the sexy lingerie that complemented her small waist and fat ass. She was 5-11 a hundred and fifty pounds and shape like an hour glass.

"How about these Baby," Gold asked while holding a pair of red thongs in his hand.

"Does it matter? Fucking with you, I'm not going to have them on long," Yalonda replied while paying for her things. After leaving Victoria's, she moved on to looking for the shoes she wanted.

It was 2:30 in the afternoon when they pulled back up to the house. Gold gave Yalonda a kiss and told her he would see her later. While pulling away from the house, he called them Crip niggas up. They met at the Pep Boys at 3:30 on the nose. Gold convinced them to sell him each key for nineteen thousand. They agreed, but only under the condition that Gold was able to grab five at a time. After a few minutes of doing the math, the deal was made. Gold went back to his spot to grab the rest of the money for the extra two keys. And made it back within 20 minutes, it was the start of a short relationship.

Gold figured that with his Larimer niggas copping how they cop and Jason's hustling ass crew, them five keys would be gone in a week. And with the shit moving that fast, the Crip niggas would have no choice but to take him to see their boss.

$

"Shameka! Bring your sexy ass in here," Jason yelled while counting about seven stacks. "Here, put this in the safe."

He handed her a wad of twenties and smacked her on her ass as she walked by. After putting the money in the safe, Shameka put her infamous fuck cd in the CD player and then laid down on the bed in the 'Ready' position. Picking up on her vibe, Jason locked the bedroom door and began to kiss and lick on her body, starting at her inner thigh. He slowly removed her skirt and panties while sliding his middle finger across her silky clit. She moaned in pleasure as his tongue ran through her pussy lips. Twenty minutes into it, Gold's voice echoed through Jason's Nextel. "Damn!" Jason replied, grabbing his phone. He removed his face from Shameka's pussy before responding, "What's up old head?"

"Yo, it's time my nigga. Meet me at your mom's in like ten minutes."

"I'm there my nigga," Jason said in an 'I'm on my way' type of manner.

"Bay, go get that money. I'll be here when you get back," Shameka stated, noticing the disgust that was written on Jason's face.

"Yeah, you better be," he said to her as he kissed her on her lips. With his peach fuzz mustache still moist from her pussy juice. After tonguing her down he headed to the bathroom to wash his face and then rolled out.

Chapter 4

Upon walking through the door, Jason saw five saran wrapped blocks on the kitchen table. Gold sat Jason down and went over the plan.

"Look, this is how we're going to do it young nigga. The drought about over right; and niggas are going to start dropping their prices. To maybe about nine or even eight." Gold paused to inhale the weed smoke. "But these niggas is greedy young nigga and that's where we going to get em'. We're making straight melt while those other niggas are going to still blow their shit out the water."

While reaching for the blunt, Jason interrupted by asking how much they should make off one of the blocks.

"Like twenty-seven thousand each. That's why you got to step your game up nigga." Gold packed four of the blocks into a duffle bag and threw one to Jason. "Hit me when you done Ike." Gold said as he dapped Jason up as he walked out the door.

Everything went as planned. They ran through them five keys in a week. That month, they saw the Crip niggas four times and about eight times the following month. The Crip nigga finally introduced Gold to the real connect. He was an older Turkish man that ran with a hit squad of goons. The connect eventually fell in love with all the money Gold was bringing him and showered him with keys on top of keys as the reward.

Jason's stash went from ten thousand to ninety-eight thousand in three months. He expanded his empire to the North Side and few other neighborhoods, opening traps in the housing projects in and around the inner city. Pumping about a half a key a week out of most of them.

Gold pretty much sat back and was only serving his Larimer niggas. He would let Jason sale the rest. Jason's crew was some young go-gettas, taking over wherever they would post at.

Over the years, Jason picked up on a few things he notice while coming up. And one thing he noticed was that a happy customer was a loyal customer. Jason was the real deal, not only was he consistent – he was loyal as well.

Jermaine was due to come home in two weeks and Jason couldn't wait. He was eager for his other half to be beside him again. Gold had set up a surprise vacation to Jamaica as Jermaine's coming home present.

$

Welcome Home...

It was 8:30 a.m. and Jason woke up after a long knight at his mom's to the smell of breakfast being cooked. Jermaine was on his way home and Roxy wanted her boy to come home to a hot, home cooked breakfast.

"Yo Ike!" A familiar voice echoed through the court. It was Jermaine walking through with a grin on his face from ear to ear. Jason thought to himself, "Finally my other half is going to be out here with me." As Jermaine walked through the court, he dapped a few niggas up that were posted in front of his mom's hallway. Before entering the hall, Jermaine noticed his dream car parked in front of the court. It was a candy apple red Mustang sitting on some gold Daytons. He thought to himself, "It's time to get it," not knowing how good Jason had been doing for himself the whole time he's been down.

The excitement in Roxy and Jason's face when Jermaine walked through the door could have brightened the Dark Age. They engaged in a group hug as Roxy released tears of joy, sobbing and saying how she was going to get her shit together. They sat and ate breakfast while Jermaine told them stories about his experiences while being locked up.

After not really eating much, Jason left the kitchen and returned with an outfit and sneaks.

"Yo bro, go throw this on and meet me outside," Jason said to his brother while handing him the stuff.

While Jermaine was getting dressed, Jason went outside to cool the leather seats of the new Mustang he bought for Jermaine. Ten minutes later Jermaine walked out the hallway, and Jason threw him the spare key.

"What whip bro?" Jermaine was scoping the numerous cars parked in front, wondering which one he'd be riding in. There was a red old school Regal sitting on some chrome Dayton's, a green beat up fiend bug, and the red Mustang that he'd seen earlier.

"Your whip nigga," Jason replied.

"Don't tell me that Mustang bro!"

"Yeah that Mustang bro!" Jason said in a confident voice.

Jermaine threw his hands up in the air and smiled while walking to his new car. After entering the car, he turned the ac off and dropped the top. Jason joined him and got in the passenger seat. Jermaine turned the music up and pulled off while letting the words from Jay Z's "I'm Feeling It" record linger in the air.

"Yo bro, it feels good being free, but being free and pushing a fat ass whip feel even better! Yo, you don't know how bad I wanted to get out here and get this money with you. I had dreams of us doing exactly what we're doing right now nigga. Riding in this same whip bro! I love this shit Ike!" Jermaine expressed his feelings to Jason as they sat at the red light on Center and Kirkpatrick.

He yelled out the car window to a shorty that stood on the side of Ham's Barber Shop. "I'm home now sexy, what up?" She smiled and waved as the car pulled off.

The twins rode around the city, showing off Jermaine's new whip, stunting and hollering at every shorty within ear length of the car.

It was 11:30 in the morning when a voice chirped out of Jason's phone. "What up youngin?"

"Yo Gold, what's up with you?"

"Shit, did Jermaine touch down yet?"

"Yeah, what up big bro," Jermaine yelled into the phone.

"What's up my young nigga? Shoot out to the crib. I got a surprise for yall."

"I don't like surprises Gold, what's up?"

"Yo Jermaine, you ain't get that tough up there nigga. Just come pass the crib. Jason, you're going to like this yo, see yall when yall get here. One."

While rolling a blunt of purple, Jason sat back and directed Jermaine to Gold's, "Hit the parkway bro. Go like you're going toward Monroeville Ike."

"But Yo, what's up with the surprises and shit bro? I did two and a half years of surprises, wondering what was going to happen next. You feel me?"

Jermaine made the tires screech as he made the right onto the parkway.

"Yeah I feel you nigga, now calm the fuck down bro! This is Gold we're talking about. Quit being so paranoid nigga! Dude got you some jewels or some shit like that for you Ike! Be cool bro, be cool," Jason replied as he took a drag of the blunt they were smoking, tapping on his brother's shoulder as if he were reassuring him that everything was good.

Jason continued, "Yo, the nigga Gold been holding us down bro. All that shit me and mom was sending you was from him. He paid for mom to go to rehab and everything bro. And on some real shit bro... Yo, make this left. But on some real shit, the two New York niggas back in the day raped mom bro, and Gold killed those niggas yo!"

"What you say nigga?" Jermaine asked, as the news almost sent him into a curb as he made the left onto Gold's street.

"Yeah bro, them niggas raped mom Ike."

A tear formed in the webs of Jermaine's eyes as the words came out of Jason's mouth. The bad news left Jermaine speechless for a while.

"My brother is back on these streets! Nigga we are going straight to the top my nigga, me and you. Bro, don't let that fuck up our day. Them niggas is dead! Now let's get it, me and you bro! Pull in this driveway."

Jason was always able to calm Jermaine down and always able to paint a picture that would help to motivate Jermaine.

"Yo, we are going to have a ball tonight!" Jason said, trying to brighten the mood.

"I know! I'm trying to fuck something nice tonight bro. Hey, what's up with little Mia? She was writing me for a minute." Jermaine asked as they pulled up in Gold's driveway.

"Yeah, I be seeing her. She be fucking with this Larimer nigga. He be selling dro and shit on the eastside."

"Oh ok, she told me she got some nigga taking care of her."

"And Lil Larry was fucking her too," Jason added as if he'd forgot.

Before they were able to ring the doorbell, Gold greeted them at the door.

While sitting in Gold's living room Jermaine couldn't stop looking at Yalonda's sexy ass. She was sitting on the couch in a tee-shirt and these little ass boy-shorts on. He couldn't help but to look.

"Yo, if you think Yalonda look good, wait until you see the ladies over here," Gold said while handing Jermaine plane tickets to Jamaica. "Welcome home little bro!"

"Okay my nigga! Ok!!! But Gold, these tickets is for today!"

"Surprise nigga!" Jason said to Jermaine, while being a little surprised himself.

"The plane leaves at nine. I'll meet yall at yall mom's crib at seven and we'll pull out from there. And Jermaine, keep your eyes off my bitch," Gold said in a playing manner.

$

Ring, Ring, Ring, Ring.

Mia's phone rang as she tried to curl her hair and she scrambled to answer it.

"Hello!"

"What's up girl?"

"Who is this?"

"Rashawnda Bitch!"

"Oh, what's up girl?"

"Guess who's home?"

"I already know. I'm getting fly for his ass right now."

"I know that's right girl! Where your dude at? You talking loud as hell bitch!"

"He's outside washing his car. He don't know I'mma be in that bitch by myself on my way to the Hill girl."

"Did you talk to Jermaine yet?"

"Naw, but I just got off the phone with Daz and she seen him pushing a red drop top girl. Him and his brother."

"Girl them are some fine ass niggas and they got that dough. I'm trying to hook up with Jason girl. You got to put in a word for me."

"I will try, but Shameka got that nigga on lock girl."

"Well, call me when you get on the Hill bitch."

"Sure will."

They ended their call as Mia set her plan to get to the Hill to see the twin in motion.

"Zoe, can I use the car today? My girl having a baby shower and I want to be able to leave when I want."

"Yeah, take my Cutty."

"I'm not driving that car bay! You've done too much shit while driving that car. I'm scared to ride with you in that damn car. Can I take the Acura pleassssse bay?"

"Go head girl. You lucky I fucks with you like that. Your ass better not get not one scratch on my rims though!"

"Now you know I drive better than you. Stop playing!"

"Yeah right, but go head bay."

"Thank You!"

"It's cool bay! Call me later."

"Ok, give me kiss," Zoe smacked her on her ass as she walked off.

$

"Damn, it's biting out this bitch," Lil Larry said to himself as he got mobbed by like seven fiends.

After serving the last fiend, Larry went to put his coke back into the mailbox. As he walked backed out the hallway, he noticed a black SS crawling up the street at the entrance of the circle. He tried to make it to the twin's mom's hall, but by the time he got to the middle of the court, the tinted windows of the SS came down and the barrel of an AK47 poked out. A masked gunman let off like fifteen shots straight at Larry before the car sped off, leaving Larry and two fiends bleeding on the pavement with multiple gunshot wounds.

A lifeless body laid in the grass in front of Roxy's hallway and Larry had passed out while trying to open the hallway door.

Roxy heard the shots and called 9-1-1. Within minutes, the police and ambulance arrived on the scene.

"Base, this is Unit 16. We're going to need homicide and the coroner dispatched to 2517 Warring Court. We have one DOA and two with multiple gunshot wounds, over," Officer Keith Lyle transmitted over the radio.

Chapter 5

While reading a Money magazine one day, Gold had decided to invest some money into the stock market. So far, everything was going as planned.

"Hello, I'm calling for a Mr. Anthony Lee."

"This is he."

"This is Mr. Lagrotta from Investment Today."

"Ok."

"I'm calling to talk to you about your portfolio."

"Ok."

"Mr. Lee, I think it would be in your best interest to split the two hundred thousand into four different stocks. My partner and I have been looking at these other three stocks that have been doing magnificent, and Mr. Lee, if everything goes as planned, you would be seeing four times the amount you put in over the next two months. This is a win-win deal for you Mr. Lee!"

"It sounds good Mr. Lagrotta, so do whatever you guys think is best."

"Mr. Lee, you're going to have a good year! I will start the paperwork and fax you the documents, you will need to sign and fax back."

"That sounds good."

"It's a pleasure working for you Mr. Lee, you have a good day!"

"You too!"

A way out of the game was starting to look possible to Gold. With both the twins home, he figured that he would eventually give the whole game to them and that his connect would consider putting the twins on and letting him walk.

Gold copped so much work off them Homewood niggas, that they eventually took him to see the connect. Then he copped off the connect so much that this Turkish mother fucker threatened to kill Gold and his family if he ever tried to quit.

$

While busting a right into the Circle, Jermaine noticed that the cops and ambulance were in front of their court.

"Yo, park right here and let's walk up," Jason said while putting his blunt out in the ashtray.

"I wonder what happened, they deep than a mother fucker."

"I don't know, but I'm calling mom right now!"

"Hello!"

"Mom, what happen?"

"Lil Larry just got shot! Yall keep yall asses wherever yall at!"

"We walking through the middle court now!"

"Well, I hope yall ain't dirty!"

"Naw, we cool. Look mom, I'm about to walk in the court now. Let me see what happened and call you back!"

The cops had a section of the court taped off where a body bag laid.

"Damn, I hope that ain't my nigga, Shit!" Jason said to Jermaine as they got closer to the court.

"What the fuck happen," Jason asked some fiend nigga that was standing across the court.

"Yo, this black car pulled up and just started shooting!"

"Who's in the body bag?"

"Spoony!"

"Oh, where is Lil Larry?"

"They rushed him to the hospital already. Hey, you got something?"

"Nigga, I should smack the shit out of you asking me some shit like that nigga! Get the fuck out of here!"

Jason pushed the fiend away from him. "Yo, what time is it?"

"3:15," Jermain replied.

"The plane leaves at what, nine?"

"Yeah!"

"Look, I'm a go to the hospital and see what's up with Lil Larry. Go to Shameka's mom's house. Tell Shameka to pack me some clothes and let her know I'm on my way to the hospital. Yo, just chill there until I get there."

"Want me to call Gold?"

"Yeah. Tell him what happen and that we'll be ready at seven."

"Aiight, I'll see you in a minute"

$

"Hello!"

"Where you at girl?"

"On my way to the Hill."

"Well you might not get to see Jermaine."

"Why, what happen?"

"Girl, Lil Larry just got shot up!"

"Lil cute ass Larry?"

"Yeah girl, police is deep as hell up here and I don't think the twins are going to be up here while it's like this!"

"Is he ok?"

"I don't know girl, but they took him to the hospital. I hope he'll be ok."

"Well I'm on my way to your house."

"Ok, see you when you get here."

"Mia!"

"What!?"

"Do you have a blunt?"

"Girl you know it. I should be pulling up in like ten minutes."

$

"Who is it?"

"Jermaine!"

"Come in boy, welcome home, where is your brother," Shameka asked in a concerned voice as she opened the door.

"He is on his way to the hospital. Lil Larry just got shot in my mom's court," Jermaine replied as he flopped down on their couch. "Oh and Jason said to pack him some clothes. We're going to Jamaica tonight. Gold is taking us for my coming home present."

Shameka's phone rang before she could respond, "Hello!"

"What's up ma? Is Jermaine there yet?"

"Yeah, he's sitting right here. Is Lil Larry ok?"

"Yeah, he'll pull through."

"That's good, where are you at now?"

"On my way to your house, is my brother there?"

"Yeah, didn't I just tell you that? So you're leaving me for a while huh?"

"Just for a few days. The nigga Gold surprised us with tickets to Jamaica."

"That was nice! Well baby, let me finish packing your clothes. I'll see you when you get here."

"Ok ma, love you."

"Love you too!"

After hanging up with Shameka, Jason called Gold.

"Yo, Lil Larry just got shot!"

"I know, I just got off the phone with Jermaine. Do you know who did it?"

"I have an idea, but I don't want to talk about it on the phone. I'll tell you later."

"That's what's up."

"Yo, instead of picking us up at my mom's, we'll be at Shameka's mom's crib."

"Word, I'll see you there at seven."

$

"What we gone do with this car Loc," T-Murder asked as he exited out the driver door.

"We gone burn that shit. We going to do it somewhere over here so the police will think a Hill nigga shot them niggas."

"Zoe, that's why I fucks with you Loc. You always got the plan already thought out."

Zoe had seen Lil Larry getting freaked by Mia one night in the club and then saw his number in her phone a few weeks ago. Zoe called the number and him and Larry had words.

"I bet you that nigga don't talk shit over that phone to nobody else," Zoe said to T-Murder as they hopped into

Zoe's Cutty that he parked on the back street where they burned the stolen SS.

$

"Aye dog, what make these niggas think we are going to keep going for this shit? These nigga been over here too mother-fucking long!" Rodney stressed to KK as they watched like four fiends come out of Jason's trap on the North Side.

"Yo Rodney, them niggas is looking out dog!"

"I don't give a fuck! Them niggas ain't from over here and they keep taking our money nigga! And I guess you just cool with that huh?"

"Naw, I'm just saying ain't none of these North Side niggas showing us no love."

"Well this shit here won't be going on much longer. I'm about to shut that shit down dog!"

$

"So baby, what's your plans while I'm gone?"

"I don't know. I have finals all week so I'll be in the house studying," Shameka replied while handing Jason his keys.

"That's what's up! You just make sure you keep my pussy tight, you hear me?"

"Yeah, and you make sure you keep my dick dry, you hear me?"

"You know I am. Well, this is Gold calling me so he must be outside. I'll call you when the plane land."

"Ok baby, have a nice trip, love you!"

"I love you too ma, call you later."

As they were leaving out the house, Jermaine couldn't help but to joke about all the love u's and shit that Jason and Shameka shared.

"Nigga she got you sprung Ike. That's crazy nigga, you really in love."

"So what, that's my baby. She holds a nigga down! And matter of fact, Shut Up and get in the car nigga!"

"Aiight nigga, I love you," Jermaine replied in a humorous way before entering the car while laughing.

As they got in the car, they both gave Gold some dap.

"So what's the word on Lil Larry?" Gold asked while handing Jason the blunt that he was puffing on.

"The doctor said he'll pull through just fine," Jason replied, taking three drags of the blunt.

"So who you think did it?" Gold asked.

"Yo, I think it was this nigga Rodney from the North Side. This nigga hate that we got that trap over there. And Larry told me he seen the nigga ride through the hood the other day."

"Oh yea, want me to put them wolves on him?"

"Naw I got it, I want to look in his eyes when he dying. I'm going to do this one myself Ike!"

"Not by yourself nigga! Remember I'm home now," Jermaine added from the backseat.

"Who's working the North Side trap right now," Gold asked.

"Spade." Jason replied.

"Do you think that nigga Rodney will try to hit the trap next?"

"I don't know. What you think I should do Gold?" Jason asked.

"Call Spade and tell him to close the trap until we get back." Gold demanded.

"Aiight!"Jason replied as he passed the blunt to Jermaine.

"But in the meantime, let's go over here and fuck all this Jamaican pussy Ikeeee," Gold stated while dapping Jermaine up and laughing.

"Yea bro don't worry about it, we'll handle that when we get back Ike," Jermaine added as he passed the blunt back to Gold.

Chapter 6

"Yo I'm trapping, what's happening," Spade rapped into his phone as he answered.

"What's up Ike?" The voice on the other end responded.

"Chilling my nigga, what's up with you?"

"On my way to the airport."

"Oh yeah, that's what's up. Where you going?"

"To Jamaica."

"I thought your crazy ass brother was coming home today?"

"He's right here."

"Let me talk to the nigga!"

"In a minute yo, Lil Larry got shot today."

"Is he alright?"

"Yeah, he'll make it, but I'm thinking that nigga Rodney did it Ike!"

"Who, that nigga from over this way?"

"Yea Yup! So what I want you to do is shut the spot down. I'll be home in a week. We'll talk about the rest when I get back."

"Damn, you fucking up my plans, but I got you Ike. One," Spade replied before pressing the end button.

"Damn, this nigga shot my man on some jealous shit! And this nigga keep disrespecting my young bitch! I'm ready to do him tonight," Spade mumbled to himself while walking to the safe they had stashed in the basement of the trap.

As Spade walked out to the car, he noticed Rodney and like three other niggas standing on the porch across the street.

"Oh that nigga think its sweet!" Spade thought as he put two shoe boxes in the trunk of the car. He wanted to run up on that nigga right then and there, but he knew it wouldn't have been wise with it being daylight and all. "I better not see that nigga tonight," He mumbled to himself as he entered the driver's side of the car.

$

"Girl this weed got me high as hell. I'm surprised Zoe's nagging ass didn't call me yet," Mia said to Rashawnda.

"I know!!! That nigga is off the hook with it. Aye bitch, did you ever give Lil Larry some of that pussy?"

"Girl yeah, I thought I told you that. That nigga cute and all, but he got to step his fuck game up girl."

"Is that why yall stopped talking?"

"Girl no, Zoe seen his number in my phone."

"What!"

"Yeah girl, he called the number and everything!"

"He didn't trip?"

"Naw, not really. He just made me get my number changed. The nigga crazy though. I wouldn't be surprised if he shot Lil Larry."

"You think?"

"I don't know but I wouldn't be surprised though!"

"Not to change the subject Mia, but the other night at the club, I was horny as hell after we got done dancing."

"After who got done dancing?"

"Me and you bitch!"

"Girl, tell me you high, what you mean you was horny?"

"I don't know how to explain it, but have you ever had thoughts of being with another girl?"

"No, not really. I mean, Jermaine wrote me and asked me that before. I thought about it and that was that."

"Well, I'm thinking if I was to get with another girl, the only one I would feel comfortable with is you."

"Girl you crazy!"

"I'm serious. One kiss Mia, just to see how it feel."

"I don't know girl, you crazy!"

"One kiss bitch, that's all!"

"Ok, one kiss." Mia said as her curiosity began to rise.

Mia sat on the couch next to Rashawnda and they both closed their eyes as their lips met. Rashawnda gently pushed her tongue between Mia's lips until she felt their tongues meet. Mia twirled her tongue around Rashawnda's before their lips separated.

"That felt good. Weird, but good," Mia said after they finished.

"I know girl, my pussy wet as hell." Rashawnda added.

"So bitch, if I ever decide to go all the way, you better be ready," Mia said as she grabbed her keys and purse off the coffee table.

"Bitch, call me tomorrow!"

"I will girl, let me go before Zoe's ass come looking for me." Mia replied as she walked out the door.

$

"We will be landing in Jamaica in approximately thirty minutes. Thanks for flying with American Airlines," the pilot announced over the intercom.

"Yo, we about to land, wake up nigga," Jason said to Jermaine as he tugged on his shirt.

"That nigga was snoring loud as hell," Gold added.

"I'm up nigga damn! I ain't sleep last night, anxious to get the fuck out of lock up and here you go waking me the fuck up!"

"We about to land nigga!"

"Aiight, call Shameka and tell her you love her or something and leave me the fuck alone!"

Gold laughed at the two talking shit to each other, reminding him of when they were younger.

$

"Where you going?" Nay asked Spade as, Spade was grabbing his gun off the dresser.

"Going to make this snap right quick. I'll be right back."

"Well bay, could you bring a blunt back in with you?"

"Yea yup bay, call you when I'm on my way back."

"Round two when you get back right?"

"Oh for sure!" Spade replied as he walked out the door.

He got in his candy apple red old school Nova and pulled off headed for the North Side.

Spade knew Rodney would be drinking at the Home Plate, a bar all the North Side niggas would go and drink at when it got slow on the block. He parked his car all the way down the street on Woodland Ave. and walked to the bar. As he got to the corner, he noticed the fiend nigga Jack standing in front of the bar.

"Yo Jack, who got that work?" Spade asked, as if he were a fiend too.

"A couple niggas. Why, you trying to get something?"

"Yeah, but I only fuck with Rodney though. Go tell him I'm on the side of the bar."

"Ok!" Jack was high as hell and actually thought Spade was a fiend.

Two minutes later, Rodney and Jack hit the corner into a hell of bullets, hitting both in multiple areas. Spade tucked the hot ass gun in his hoody and jogged to his whip.

With it being so dark on Woodland, nobody really saw Spade as he jogged to his car. He got in and calmly proceeded back to the Hill. A little nervous as he drove pass a fleet of police cars on their way to the crime scene, Spade tossed the gun over the Roberto Clement Bridge as he rode across it.

$

"In today's news, it was a bloody June 2nd in the city of Pittsburgh yesterday. Two separate shootings left three dead and two wounded. The first shooting occurred in the 2400 block of Warring Court in the Hill District, at approximately 3:00 in the evening. Dave Matts, 47 of Bloomfield, was pronounced dead at the scene. The other two victims' names have not been released. The police have no suspects at this time. The second shooting occurred on Woodland Avenue on the city's North Side. 41 year old Jack Reems, and 26 year old

Rodney Battles, were both found on the side of the Home Plate bar, located at the corner of Shadeland and Woodland Avenue, both with multiple gunshot wounds. They both died a short time later at Allegheny General Hospital. The police have no suspects for this shooting as well, but believe the two shootings are not connected. We will have more on these stories at 11."

"Bay, you be careful out there today. The police are probably going crazy. Three niggas got killed yesterday and it's going to be hot!" Mia said to Zoe as he walked into the room.

"I'm chilling anyway. Did you catch the names?"

"Yeah Rodney, Dave and Jack."

"Oh, well I don't know anybody by those names," Zoe replied as he sat on the edge of the bed.

He started rubbing his hand across Mia's ass, trying to get her ready for a second go, but Mia was thinking of the kiss she shared with Rashawnda last night, not really noticing that he was even touching her.

"Damn baby, you act like you don't feel me rubbing on your ass," Zoe said, smacking her on the cheeks of her fat, plump bottom.

While pulling his dick closer to her face, Mia replied, "Let me show you how much I feel you!" She gently put it between her lips and extended her tongue, twirling it around the head. The way Mia sucked on his dick had Zoe fucked up and had him willing to kill whoever tried to come between that good head of hers.

$

"Yo, who you think killed Rodney dog," Drama asked KK as they stood on the corner waiting on the afternoon rush to start jump off.

"I don't know dog, but when I find out who it was, I'm definitely going to make them join him!" KK replied while tapping his hand on the Glock 45 he had tucked in his pants.

"Yo, I think that Hill nigga got something to do with it," Drama replied.

"You think so? He did look at us funny as hell yesterday when we were on the porch. Yo, if he did or didn't do it, I'm going to murk dude next time I see him. That's my word dog," KK said while puffing his blunt.

$

"Yo, where Jermaine at Ike?" Gold asked Jason as he entered the hotel room.

"I think he's down the hall with that one bitch from last night. You know that nigga haven't had no pussy in two and a half years. He was going hard last night Ike!"

"So what you saying, you didn't get no pussy nigga?"

"Naw, I got some head off that one bitch I was dancing with though!"

"So what's up for today?"

"I don't know. I'm trying to rent some jet ski's or something though."

"Shit, me too! I got to make a few calls and then it's whatever."

"I know, I got to call Shameka's crazy ass before she be tripping. I was supposed to call her when our plane touched."

"Alright then nigga, I'll be back in a minute."

They dapped each other up as Gold bounced to his own room to handle his business.

"Yo!" Jason replied as Shameka answered her phone.

"I've been waiting on you to call. Spade has been calling me all morning. He was trying to get me to give him your other number."

"Oh yeah! For what?"

"He wouldn't say."

"Alright, I'll call him. So what's up with you?"

"Tired. Been arguing with my mom all night."

"For what?"

"I think she wants her space. We need to find us an apartment or something bay."

"Yeah, I was thinking the same thing. Well start looking and when I get back, we can go check out some of the spots you found."

"Ok, so how are you liking Jamaica?"

"It's alright. It would have been better with you here with me."

Blushing, Shameka replied, "You better not be fucking with none of them nasty bitches!"

"You ain't got to worry about that ma, these hoes ain't shit out here!"

"Whatever!"

"Real shit ma, but let me hit Spade and I'll hit you later."

"Alright, Love you."

"Love you too ma."

After hanging up the phone, Jason thought about how lucky he was to have such an understanding girl. He then refocused his attention and called up Spade.

"Yo, what's up Ike?" Spade said as he answered in an excited voice.

"Same shit my nigga. What's up with you Ike, did you shut the spot down like I asked you Ike?"

"Yeah my nigga and I handled old boy already."

"You did what?!"

"I took care of old boy."

"Spade, we weren't even sure if homey even did it. I said I think dude had something to do with it! Yo, don't let me find out you did dude cause he fucking your young bitch! This ain't good Spade!" Jason stressed.

"Dog, I thought you would be alright with it nigga! Now you don't have to get your hands dirty Ike!"

"Al-right nigga!!! Yo this shit's crazy, look don't go back on the North. Stay in the hood until I get back. Yo, and knock the rest of that shit in weight. Spade, you know you're my nigga right."

"For sure Ike!" Spade answered

After hanging up the phone, Jason rolled a big ass blunt of the best Jamaica had to offer.

While enjoying his blunt, he thought about Lil Larry and if the nigga Rodney really had something to do with him getting shot. "Rodney, Rodney, Rodney...Why? I tried to look out for all you North Side niggas and this how yall repay me, by shooting my man." This shit just doesn't add up. I need to talk to Gold about this. He'll know how I should handle this shit. I really don't think it was the nigga Rodney that shot Little Larry, but maybe that's because Spade ended up doing it and I wanted to do it myself." After a few moments of silence and the light sound of the fire on the blunt burning, Jason realized he was talking to his self. Trying to make sense of all the bull shit.

He had this conversation with himself while smoking on his blunt, trying to make sense of everything that was going on.

$

After giving Zoe the best head he ever had in his life, Mia was trying to find her way back to the lips of Rashawnda. "Zoe, what are we doing today? I wanted to go to the mall." Mia wined.

"I don't know Bay, I got a lot of shit to handle today."

"Well I'm not sitting in this house all day. When you leave, I'm leaving."

"Bay, I didn't even say I was going anywhere. Didn't you tell me it was going to be hot? I got some shit to handle, but it can be handled from the house. If you want to go outside, take the whip and I'll call you if I need you."

"You sure Bay? Do you want me to stay in with you?" Mia asked hoping he would say no.

"Naw, you cool. I'll call you later." Her plan worked she thought to herself as she smiled on her way out the door.

$

"Yo, let me hit that blunt Ike," Jermaine said as he walked through the door. Jason welcomed Jermaine's presence, but not his jolly demeanor.

"You're in a happy mood on a fucked up day."

"Jason, how could it be a fucked up day when I just got out of the best pussy I ever had in my life Ike!"

"Oh yeah, I got to hit her girl before we leave, but yo, Spade murked the nigga that I thought shot Lil Larry."

"Did you give the word?"

"Naw!"

"Well why is niggas making moves without your approval?" Jermaine asked as he passed Jason the blunt back.

"Spade's a hot head yo!"

"Well we're going to have to cool him down when we get home, but right now, leave that shit at the crib. We're here to have fun my nigga!"

"Yeah, you right bro." Jason replied.

Chapter 7

"Yo, it feels good then a mother-fucker to be back in the Burgh!"

"I know, but Jermaine, your homecoming present is over. It's time to get this money! I got to figure out where we need you." Jason stated.

"Where yall need me! Nigga, I'm your new right hand. You need me right next to you! I know you didn't think I was coming home to run a nigga's block! Look Jason, I'm your twin Ike, what's yours is mine and what's mine is yours – don't change up on me now bro!"

"I could never change on you bro, you're a part of me. I'm just saying I got to put you down on how things work. That's all my nigga. We going to sit down and put it all together when we get to my crib. I mean Shameka's mom's crib..."

Gold was sleep in the backseat of the car, dreaming about the twenty room mansion he planned to buy once he got out of the game. While pulling up to Shameka's house, Jason reached back to wake him up.

"Yo, you cool to drive Ike?" Jason asked.

"So are you ready to re-up buck?" Ignoring Jason's question with one of his own, Gold got out and made his way to the driver seat.

"I think so. I got a few pick-ups to make so I'll call you around noon and I should be ready."

"Al-right just call me. Jermaine, you have fun freaky ass young nigga? You probably hit the whole Jamaica," Gold shouted out the window as he pulled off.

$

"What's up baby? I'm about to pull up." Gold said as Linda answered her phone.

"Well why you call? It's like five in the morning and you calling like you don't have a key."

"You didn't know I was coming back today and I didn't know if you had a nigga in there, you feel me."

"Yeah, but Gold you know I don't bring niggas to my crib. If they can't afford a room, they can't afford this pussy."

"Yea, yea, you right ma. Well I'll be there in like five minutes."

"Alright, see you when you get here baby," Linda said in a tired voice before hanging up the phone.

Linda was one of Gold's main bitches. She was down for whatever. Unlike Yalonda, Gold could get Linda to do almost anything. She was what you called a ride or die bitch for real. Her and Gold have been cool for years. She figured she had the upper hand as Gold's main side bitch because she got just as much out Gold as Yalonda did and still was able to have fun with other niggas.

"What's up girl," Gold asked Linda as he smacked her on her ass.

"Sleep nigga!" Linda replied.

"Aye, who's that in the living room?"

"My girl Jen. We went out last night and she was too drunk to drive home."

"Oh, is that her Benz out front?"

"Yeah, well her man's Benz, but he just got three to six up state."

"Oh yeah! That's the nigga Ricky's young bitch. You know I fucked her last year bay?"

"Yeah, she told me." Linda replied while cutting Gold a evil eye.

"Oh word, well come here and bless your nigga bay." Gold demanded as he laid back on the bed.

Linda rolled over and got on top of him. She pleaded for him not to do it hard so Jen wouldn't hear them, but Jen hearing them was part of Gold's plan.

$

"Yo, be quiet bro, I'm not trying to wake up Shameka's mom." Jason demanded as him and Jermaine sat in Shameka's mom's living room.

"My bad Ike, I'm going to catch a quick hour or two on this couch."

"That's what's up. I'll wake you up when I'm ready."

Jermain laid on the couch as Jason headed back to Shameka's room. When he opened the door, he noticed Shameka was sleeping with nothing on. After closing the door behind him, Jason removed his clothes and leaned over her. He began to lick right below her right butt cheek, startling Shameka at first. Noticing it was Jason, she turned over on her back and he began to lick right above her clit, proceeding down her pussy lips. She moaned as he pleased her.

$

After filling Linda up with cum Gold decided he was going to go check out Jen. "Bay, I'm going to get some water, you want something?"

"No thanks but put your boxers on. I told you Jen out there."

"That girl drunk sleep. I'll be right back."

Ass whole naked, Gold went to the kitchen. As he got his water, he couldn't help but to notice how sexy Jen looked. She was sleep with one leg on the top of the couch showing the bunched up crouch of her pink Victoria panties. Even after just fucking Linda, the sight turned him on. Gold knew Linda wouldn't have a problem with him fucking Jen. Shit, she probably would want to join in.

"Nigga, I knew you were coming out here to see if she was woke!"

"Bay, I came to get some water, but shorty do look sexy as hell on that couch like that."

Linda sat at the kitchen table not willing to let a sleeping Jen get all of Golds attention. So while Gold was fucking Jen with his eyes, Linda put his dick inside her mouth. A few minutes into it, Gold's moans woke Jen up.

"Linda, is that you girl?"

"Yeah, it's me."

"What you doing in there?"

"Fucking with Gold's crazy ass."

"Oh, Hi Gold!"

"What's up little ma?"

Jen wasn't able to see that Gold was naked. She got herself together and got off the couch and started to walk to the kitchen. When she got close to the half of wall that separated the kitchen from the living room, she noticed Linda giving Gold head.

"Yall are crazy!" Jen said while shaking her head.

"Girl, don't act like you never sucked dick before!" Linda stated as she briefly removed Gold's dick from her mouth.

"Not in the middle of the kitchen." Jen replied.

"No disrespect little ma, but come join us," Gold asked while stroking himself in front of Linda's face. Jen wasn't sure if she wanted to but the sight of Linda sucking his dick turned her on, so she proceeded into the kitchen.

As she got close to Gold, Linda started to rub Jen's ass. Gold and Jen started kissing while Linda continued to suck his dick. After a few minutes of Gold sucking on Jen's tongue, she got down and started licking all that wouldn't fit in Linda's mouth. Gold moaned as they took turns putting him in and out of each other's mouth. Threesomes wasn't new to Gold, but have one with these two was truly unexpected.

Chapter 8

"Yo, I just got word on where the nigga Spade live at."

"Yeah?"

"Yeah, he's staying with this little bitch up Robinson Court on the Hill."

"Yo, you know that spot be cracking like all the time yo! There won't be anywhere to lay on that nigga."

"Yeah, you right, but I was thinking we shoot up the whole court and continue to do so until we luck up and kill that nigga!"

"Shit yo, that sounds like a plan. Fuck it, let's do it," Dog Eye replied to KK as they followed a line of cars out of the cemetery.

$

"Yo, wake up nigga," Jason said to Jermaine as he walked in the living room.

"Damn, what time is it?"

"It's like 12. We got to get this money nigga, come on."

"Here I come Ike. Let me piss real quick."

"Aiight, I'll be in the car. Tell Shameka to close the door and lock it behind you."

Sitting in the car, Jason rolled a blunt while waiting on his brother.

"Yo, I need a phone Ike," Jermaine said as he was getting in the car.

"We'll go get you one in a minute, but right now we got to collect this money. Gold's ready to re-up today and I got to go look at some houses with Shameka later."

"Ok, well I'm going to go fuck with Mia's sexy ass while you go look at them cribs. See if shorty going give me some of that head."

"Larry said that head off the hook."

"Oh yeah, Larry got that head?"

"Yeah Yup bro. Well that's what he told me."

"Well after we collect this money, drop me off at her spot."

"Got you Ike, now let's get this money!"

While riding to collect, Jason told Jermaine his plans. Jason wanted to have a million dollars by the time he was twenty one. They would be eighteen in July and had a little over two-hundred thousand. Gold was giving Jason five bricks at a time at twenty-thousand a piece. He would sell three wholesale at twenty-eight a piece and grind the other two for about thirty-two each. That was like forty-eight thousand that Jason would profit every flip, but he was ready to expand his hustle. That's where Jermaine fit in.

"Yo, what's up with that nigga you told me about that got the dope connect?" Jason asked Jermaine as he he handed him the blunt.

"Oh, I got to stop pass his sister's crib to get his number, but the word is dude doing it real big."

"Oh yeah, well we got to see that nigga. I got a few niggas that be moving that dope like crazy."

"Ok, well I got us. I'll stop pass her house tomorrow," Jermaine replied to Jason as he exhaled the smoke out of his lungs.

After collecting off the small time workers, they were on their way to collect and talk to Spade about what happened on the North Side last week. As they pulled up into R.C. which was short for Robinson Court, Jason noticed the nigga KK ride pass in a green Impala.

"That was them North Side niggas! Yo, let's hurry up in this nigga's crib. I don't know what them niggas is on." Jason said as he pulled into the parking lot.

Jason and Jermaine spoke to the niggas that was sitting in front of Spade's hall and proceeded into the hallway.

"Who was that Bro?" Jermaine asked as they walked up the steps to Spade's crib.

"That nigga Rodney's man KK. They got to be on some other shit."

After entering Spade's crib...

"Yo nigga, how it feel to be home? You get some pussy yet nigga?" Spade asked Jermaine as they all stood in the living room.

"Did I? I just got back from Jamaica. I fucked some pussy that you could only dream about brick head mafucka," Jermaine answered back, capping on Spade's big ass head as they gave each other a hug.

While the three went and sat at the kitchen table to talk, they all suddenly hit the floor after hearing at least twenty-four gunshots out in the court.

"Yo, what the fuck?" Jason said as he reached for the gun that was on his waist.

"That nigga KK yo!"

"What about him," Spade asked.

"We just seen that nigga ride through. I knew them niggas was on some other shit! Yo Spade, bring that money to my girl's crib. I'm getting out of here before the Jakes come."

Jason and Jermaine jogged pass two of the niggas they dapped up who were shot and now laying on the ground. After hopping in the whip, Jason sped off, hoping to make it out of R.C. before the police arrived.

$

"Yo, I seen that nigga Jason walking into the court before we started dumping."

"Yeah, well, this shit will be on the news later. Hopefully we hit that nigga!"

KK and Dog Eye ditched the car on a back street on the Hill and walked to their car, nice and calm like nothing ever happened.

$

"Yo, that shit was crazy! I'm going to kill that nigga KK!" Jermaine said as he frantically looks around to see if the police was coming.

"I know. The crazy shit is we tried to look out for them North Side niggas. And now they want a war. Well I got a war for them niggas Ike!"

Jason and Jermaine were hysterical as they rode back to Shameka's house. Jermaine wasn't home two weeks and was getting shot at already.

"Yo, let me see your phone bro," Jermaine said as they pulled up beside his whip.

"Who you calling Ike?" Jason asked.

"Mia, trying to see what's up with shorty. See if I could get some head or something. I need something to take my mind off of what just happened. I ain't used to this shit yet bro!"

"Well get used to it cause we got some work to put in. Them niggas got to go!"

"Yeah, they do… Hello?"

"Who is this?"

"Jermaine girl. Where you at?"

"At the crib. Let me call you right back, or then again, do you know where Rashawnda live?"

"Yeah, by my mom's crib right?"

"Yeah, meet me there in like an hour."

"Aiight. One."

After pressing the end button on the phone, Jermaine dapped his brother up and got into his car. "What you about to do Bro?"

"Wait on Spade to bring this money and then call Gold."

"Oh aiight then. I'll be up by mom's crib."

"Be safe up there Bro. Love you. One," Jason replied before Jermaine sped off.

$

"Girl, Jermaine is on his way to your house. Let him chill until I get there."

"Oh ok," Rashawnda replied to Mia before hanging up her phone.

Rashawnda, thought to herself that this might be a good time to get more than a kiss off of Mia. She has been dreaming about making out with Mia for a few weeks, and now may be her chance. While she was thinking, there was a knock at the door.

"Who is it," she yelled as she squeezed her fat ass into these tight ass shorts.

"Jermaine ma. Mia asked me to meet her here."

"Oh ok, one minute!"

Rashawnda opened the door and greeted Jermaine in. One look at Rashawnda's ass and Jermain instantly wanted to fuck her. Little did he know, she instantly wanted to fuck him to.

"Hi you doing today ma?"

"Fine and you? I know you're happy to be home."

"Yes, I am and never trying to go back."

"I know that's right! Well make yourself at home. Mia should be here shortly."

"That's what's up. I got this purp. You smoke bay?"

"Yeah, but Mia should be pulling up in a minute. Let's wait on her."

"Oh, aiight then, that's what's up."

Jermaine and Rashawnda sat in the living room talking and getting to know each other. Jermaine was locked up when Rashawnda moved to the Hill, so they had never met. She was more of his type than Mia, being that she was thick and all, but Mia was pretty, slim and sexy as fuck. He thought it was going to become a problem because he was definitely attracted to both of them.

$

"Yo, where you at Ike?"

"In the crib. Why, what's wrong, you ready?"

"Naw. I'm waiting on Spade to bring this money. But yo, them North Side niggas just shot at us Ike!"

"Oh Yeah!"

"Hell Yeah. I'm going over there and let them niggas have it!"

"Naw, don't even worry about it Bro. Just get me them nigga's names and I'm a put the goons on them. You don't need to get caught up in that bullshit. I thought you and Shameka was going to look at some spots?"

"We about to leave in a minute. Yo, I'm going to leave the bag of money with Shameka's mom so just stop pass whenever you ready."

"Word! I'll talk to you later Bro, be safe!"

"No doubt, One."

As Jason pushed the end button on his phone, Spade was at the door. They sat and talked as Jason counted the money. He informed Spade that Gold was going to handle the whole North Side situation so they wouldn't have to worry about the shit no more. All they had to worry about was how they were going to make up the money they were going to miss by closing the North Side trap. Spade told Jason he was looking at this spot on the Eastside that be biting.

$

"Hey baby, welcome home!" Mia said to Jermaine as she walked in Rashawnda's house.

"Hey sexy! You don't know how bad I've been wanting to see you in person," Jermaine replied as they hugged each other. Mia blushed as Jermaine's hands rubbed back and forth on her ass.

"Ok love birds, roll that purp up!"

The three sat and smoked while Jermaine and Mia reminisced about the old times. After feeling the effect of the weed, Rashawnda went into her room, returning with three ecstasy pills.

"Hey, you trying to pop?"

Jermain looked up and noticed what she was talking about and couldn't believe his eyes.

"Naw baby, that shit ain't for me but I wouldn't judge what yall do."

"So, what's up Mia? You popping with me girl?"

Mia popped a few times but didn't like how it made her feel the next day. She really wanted to be open for whatever Jermaine wanted her to do since she'd been wanting to fuck him for a few years now, and she wanted it to be the best he ever had.

"Yeah girl, get me some water. A big glass of water."

$

"So, are you ready babe?" Shameka asked Jason as she walked into the living room.

"Yeah, can you ask your mom to hand this bag to Gold when he come pass?"

After she gave her mom the bag, they left to go look at the house she found. It was a three bedroom, two bathroom house which sat in a wooded area out North Hills.

They talked about the shooting earlier and Shameka stressed to Jason how she was starting to get scared. All the shootings and drug activity was starting to make her nervous. Jason promised her that once they move, he wouldn't bring none of the shit around her. Shameka had two more years to finish nursing school and figured if she was able to get Jason to take some type classes, that they would be able to live a decent life.

$

Mia was now feeling the effect of the pill. Her pussy was wet as hell and she was growing hornier and hornier by the minute. Rashawnda told Mia and Jermaine that her head was starting to spin and that she was going to lie down for a minute.

Soon as Rashawnda left the room, Mia started to rub Jermaine's dick through his pants.

"Wow Jermaine, you are so big," she stated in a sexy voice as she started to zip his zipper down.

"Oh yeah, you like it big huh ma?"

"Yes I do!" Mia replied as she stuffed his dick as far down her throat as she could.

"Ohhhh, shit yeah ma! Do what you do baby," Jermaine moaned as Mia slurped and licked all over his dick.

She gave him head for about twenty minutes before noticing Rashawnda was standing by the kitchen watching. Mia ignored her presence as she continued to please Jermaine's love pole. While Mia was sucking on him, he couldn't help but to notice Rashawnda standing by the entrance of the living room, rubbing her pussy. He knew from that moment it was going to be a lot of freaking in there today.

Jermaine motioned to Rashawnda to come to him. As she got closer, Mia lifted her head off of his dick and began licking Rashawnda's stomach. He stood up as they started to kiss and undo each other's clothes.

They all licked, sucked and fucked as the New Jack City soundtrack banged from the twelve inch woofers Rashawnda had hooked up to her system. The lyrics to Color Me Badd sang through the speakers:

"Tick tock you don't stop...to the tick tock you don't stop...to the tick tock you don't stop...to the tick tock you don't stop... Ooohoohoohoohooh... Oohoohoohoohoohooh... Oohoohoohoohoohooh... Hey, beautiful lady... I need you, tonight...Lovely lady – I want to make you feel alright yeah... Oohoohoohoohoohooh... I can't deny baby... I want to love you down...Oohoohoohoohoohooh... You are so fine baby – and I want to do is... Ooohoohoohoohoohooh... I want to sex you up ... All night...You make me feel good... Oohoohoohoohoohooh ... I want you by my side... Oohoohoohoohoohooh... I want to sex you up... Say do you feel lonely girl...Let me turn down the lights...so I could hold you in the darkness... Oh baby, let's make love tonight yeah... Oohoohoohoohoohooh – You feel so right baby...when I love you down... Please be my wife sugar...cause all I want to do is...Ooohoohoohoohoohooh... I want to sex you up...Oohoohoohoohoohooh... I want to sex you up"

As the words hit Jermaine's ears, He was getting more and more turned on, looking down at these two beautiful ladies doing their thing on his dick at the same damn time. The shit was feeling so good that he started singing those tunes his-damn-self. "I want to sex you up! All night, Yeah! Ooh-ooh-ooh-ooh-ooh"

$

"Baby, I really like this house!"

"Yeah, I like it too Bay. You think the lady would like to sell it?"

"Baby, we were supposed to be looking to rent."

"I know, but if you really like it, we should try to buy it."

"Baby, you're only seventeen. I don't even think you're old enough to buy a house."

"Maybe not, but your mom could, or Gold will do it for me."

"Yeah, you're right. Well, you call Gold and I'm going to call the lady." The way Shameka and her mother had been arguing lately, she didn't think it would be a good idea to put anything in her name.

As the two of them sat on the porch, they both started to dial out on their cell phones.

$

"Yalonda, could you get me that duffle bag out of the basement bay," Gold asked as his phone rang.

"Hello!"

"What's up old head?"

"Shit. Putting this money together. What's wrong Ike?"

"Nothing! I wanted to know if you could put this crib in your name for me?"

"I thought yall was going to rent the spot?"

"We was, but Shameka like it and it's out the way so I figured, shit, we might as well buy it."

"What they want for it?"

"Don't know yet, but by the look of it, probably like a hundred g's."

"That's a lot for your first crib Ike, but if you want it, I got you Ike. Let me know."

"Aiight. Shameka's on the phone with the lady now. I'll call you later."

"Yo, what's them niggas names that shot at yall?"

"Oh, I don't know their real names, but it was the nigga KK and I think the nigga with him was Dog Eye."

"Ok, I'm on it. Don't worry about it, One." Gold assured Jason that everything would be taken care of before ending the call.

Shameka ended her call and updated Jason, "She said she would definitely be interested in selling it Baby."

"Well that's what's up. Gold said he will put it in his name, so we good. Are you sure you like it? Because once we pay for it, that's it."

"Yes, I'm sure. The lady said she could meet us tomorrow," Shameka replied showing her happiness with a big smile. Jason had just made Shameka the happiest girl in the world.

Chapter 9

"Goldie, how's it hanging?" Akbatu greeted Gold as he walked through the door.

"It's hanging Akbatu, it's hanging! Here go the money, and I need a favor from you." Gold said as he tossed the duffle bag on the couch and sat down.

"Favor, what type of favor Goldie?" Akbatu asked.

"I got a problem with a couple guys from the North Side. I was hoping I could borrow your goons."

"Sure Goldie, sure my friend. Just tell me their names and it's handled. Goldie, you know I'll do anything for my top notch Pittsburgh worker. You know how much money you make me?"

"Yeah I do. That's why I'm hoping you let me exit out the game while I'm on top."

"Now Goldie, you know I can't do that! But you know what Goldie, if you find me someone that can move as much work as you do, I will let you out." Akbatu said as he handed Gold a duffle bag full of coke.

"Remember you said that Akbatu, remember you said that." Gold replied as he walked out the door.

Akbatu just gave Gold his way out of the game. An out, that Gold would take advantage of soon. He figured he would just pay for Jason's house so Jason would have enough dough to meet Akbatu's demands, which was two-hundred thousand a flip.

As much as Gold cared for the twins, he wanted to get out of the game more than anything. A few months ago, his lawyer told him that the FBI has been asking about him and that he should really think about stopping. But stopping wasn't as easy as his lawyer thought. Everything was starting to look brighter for Gold though, because now he *has* a way out.

$

"Hey Josh, get a couple guys together and take care of these guys for me," Akbatu handed Josh a piece of paper with the names KK and Dog Eye on it. "You should be able to find them on the North Side. And Josh, send their parents their hands."

Josh was good at what he do, and that was putting together gruesome homicides. He gathered his team and headed for the North Side.

They left the hotel in two Impalas laced with cop lights inside of them. Akbatu's goons were all illegal aliens with no way for the police to trace them.

Josh was the only survivor when a Turkish mob killed his whole family. His father was involved with smuggling teenage girls into different countries and one of the girls happened to be the niece of the boss of the

Turkish Mob. The police found Josh in his living room barely alive, surrounded by the corpses of his family. He survived three gunshot wounds, one to the head, and two to the chest. They had cut his brother's neck from ear to ear, shot his mother in the face, all while his father watched as he was chained to a chair, before eventually cutting his neck too.

After recovering, Josh was sent to a military school where he developed into a young killer for the Turkish Army. Akbatu, was a former colonel for the army and decided to put him a gang together along with an American immigrant by the name of Paul and headed for the U.S., bringing Josh and six other young killers with him.

$

"Damn ladies, what did I do to deserve this? Yo, this was the best coming home present ever! Like real shit ma!" Jermaine said as he kissed Mia's back, out of breath and fatigued, he pulled out of her as she lifted her head out of Rashawnda's crouch.

Jermaine and the ladies sat and smoked a blunt, all three amazed at what had just taken place. It was the first threesome for all of them. Mia was a little ashamed but didn't regret it, not one bit of it.

"Mia, let me find out you did this before!"

"Why you say that?"

"Because I never got my pussy licked like that!"

"Girl, I just did what I felt you doing to me."

They both laughed as Jermaine butted in saying, "Did yall plan this shit because this all happened too easy."

Mia cut an eye at Rashawnda saying, "I think *somebody* did."

"Well if yall did or didn't, I'm glad it happened."

As they were talking, Mia quickly signaled for everybody to shut up because Zoe was calling her phone.

"Hello!"

"Where you at bay?"

"Up Rashawnda's."

"Oh, what time you think you'll be home?"

"I don't know. My mom wanted me to stay at her house so I could watch my little sister."

"Oh ok, well I'm going out so you got to switch me cars."

"Aiight, well I'll be here whenever you're ready to come get it. I know one thing, you better not be out there fucking with no hoes!"

"Shit, you already know what it is," Zoe replied while laughing.

"Yeah ok!" Mia replied back before pressing the end button on her phone.

$

It was now like seven in the evening and Jermaine was still at Rashawnda's. Jason and Shameka were just waking up from a nap. Gold was at his spot separating the bricks. Zoe had already switched cars with Mia. KK was at his shorty's crib playing Madden on the X-Box and the boy Dog Eye was on his way to the Home Plate.

Jason explained to Shameka that he would be going to see Gold in a few minutes. Jermaine was knocked out on Rashawnda's couch, while her and Mia rolled big ass blunts of his weed. And the night was starting to wind down.

Jason met Gold at his spot. After handing Jason seven bricks, he informed him that the North Side niggas would be getting the business tonight and to make sure he was around somebody, just in case he needed an alibi.

Jason went to Rashawnda's after dropping the work off at his mom's. As he walked into the hall, he could smell the strong scent of some purp being blazed up. The smell got stronger and stronger as he walked up the steps. Before he could knock Rashawnda opened the door and greeted him with a big ass smile on her face.

"Hey Jason!" She said as he walked into her living room.

"What's up ma, what the hell did yall do to my brother?" Jason asked after noticing Jermaine stretched out on Rashawnda's couch.

"Just gave him the best night of his life," Mia said while giggling.

"Oh yeah, that's what's up! He needed it after the morning we had today. Well, I'm not going to wake him. I see he's in good hands," Jason stated with a smile on his face. "Tell him to call me in the morning."

"Ok, I will," Mia replied as Jason walked out the door.

$

"Josh, what about that bar… Um, what's the name of it, the Home…?"

"What, the Home Plate?" Josh answered finishing Peter's sentence

"Yes, yes, the Home Plate. A lot of young niggers hang out in that bar."

$

"Yo mama, let me get another Goose straight up," Dog Eye said to the bar maid as he sat at the bar. It was like his seventh shot. He was trying to get drunk, cause that was the only time he was able to forget about what him and KK did earlier that day.

Dog Eye talked a good game, but wasn't really a killer. He sat at the bar nervous as hell thinking about what him and KK did that afternoon. He thought at any minute the police was going to roll up in the bar and arrest him.

He got so nervous, he decided to leave and go fuck one of his shorty's. As he walked out the door, he saw two narc cars sitting on the corner, his heart was thumping as he stood undecided on what way to walk. He didn't want to look suspicious so he walked in the same direction of the cars.

"Excuse me sir?"

"Who, me?"

"Yes, you, let me talk to you for a minute."

"What did I do," Dog Eye asked the officer as he walked up to the car.

"You know what you did," the officer said as he hopped out the car and grabbed him. "What's your name son?"

"Lonny Rivers!"

"No, what do your little gangbanger friends call you?"

"Um, um..."

"They call you Dog Eye, don't they?"

"Yeah, but I haven't done anything!" He said as he started to cry.

"Well, we have a warrant for your arrest." The officer cuffed him and put him in the back of the police car. "Look, we know you weren't the one that did the shooting and we'll cut you lose if you help us get KK."

Nervous and scared, Dog Eye contemplated if he wanted to snitch on KK.

"Look son, we could just put it on you and be done with it. It's up to you, you fucking nigger," The officer's partner stated.

"Ok, Ok... He's over his girlfriend's house. She stay on Pennsylvania Avenue. I know he's there because I just talked to him."

"Ok, good! See, helping yourself wasn't so hard now, was it?"

"Ok, let's go get the little nigger," the partner said as they pulled off.

"But I thought yall said yall would let me go if I told yall where he was," Dog Eye said in protest. He didn't want to be with them when they picked up KK. He knew it would be off with his head if niggas from the hood found out he snitched.

"We are son, but we need you to get him out of the house."

As they drove, Dog Eye was starting to feel a little better knowing they were going to let him go, but he still felt a tad uneasy about setting KK up to be arrested. He wasn't built for jail and almost went crazy when he was sent to Shuman Center two years ago. The judge felt sorry for him at his sentencing hearing due to the fact that he cried from the time he walked into the courtroom, to the time he walked out. The judge talked shit to him and sentenced him to house arrest.

"Right here," Dog Eye said as they rode pass Asha's house. "That blue house right there."

"Ok son, I'm going to get out and walk up to the house. When I get on the porch, you call him and tell him that you're outside. And look little nigger – If you try anything funny, I'm going to shoot you right here," the partner said as he pointed his gun at Dog Eye.

Frightened at the barrel of a gun staring in his face, he replied in a voice laced with panic, "Ok, I'm not going to try anything funny!"

He dialed KK's number and KK's call tune began to sing in his ear, "I smell pussy...is that you Irv...I smell pussy...is that you Ja...I smell pussy...is that you Black...I smell pussy...is that you Ty...Yall niggas is pussy...I'm balling now nigga, now watch me...Ain't nothing yall could do to stop me... yall niggas get so emotional...yall remind me of my bitch." 50 Cent's "I Smell Pussy" played in Dog Eye's ear as he waited for KK to answer.

"Hello!" KK answered in an aggravated tone cause when he reached for his phone the computer scored a touchdown on him.

"Yo, you still over Asha's?"

"Yeah, why what's up?"

"I'm on the porch. I got to tell you something and I don't want to say it over the phone Bro."

"Aiight, here I come Bro." KK pressed the end button on his phone and started for the front door.

As KK walked onto the porch, he was greeted by a big white man with a gun pointed to his head.

"Police! Freeze!" The man on the porch said as he grabbed and put hand cuffs on him.

$

As Jason walked through Shameka's mom's door, he was greeted by the smell of baked chicken. Hungry and tired, he spoke to Shameka's mom and proceeded to her room.

"Hey baby, did you take care of your business?"

"Yeah, I mean, not for real, I just put that shit in my mom's. I didn't feel like touching it tonight. Bay I'm tired."

"Ok, well let me make your plate. I know you got to be hungry."

"Yeah I am Bay. I'm going to take a shower first, ok?"

"Go head… You got clean underwear in that bag on the floor."

As Jason got in the shower, Shameka went and made his plate. Ms. Bell cut a jealous eye at her daughter as she watched her make Jason's plate. Ms. Bell couldn't stand to see her daughter be a better woman in the sense of taking care of a man. Ms. Bell was nice looking, but couldn't hold on to a man to save her life. The best guy she ever had was Shameka's dad and he left because all she ever did was accuse him of shit he wasn't doing. After the birth of Shameka, he split.

That was twenty years ago and Ms. Bell been through about twenty niggas ever since. Shameka's dad would come and get her every weekend and built a strong bond between the both of them. A bond that Ms. Bell despised of even until this day.

"Damn, did you give him enough?"

"What are you talking about mom?"

"That big ass plate! You didn't buy none of that food. Shit, that's why I want you to go. You and your man are eating me out of house and home."

"Mom, you are so damn jealous of me and don't even know why, but you don't have to worry about it. I'll be out by next week, sheesh!"

Shameka was fired up as she walked back to her room. She was tired of the jealousy. She loved her mother and couldn't understand why she envied her so much.

"What's wrong Bay," Jason asked when she walked in the room, noticing the sad look in her face.

"My mom gets on my nerves! Like, I swear Babe, we got to get out of this house!"

"Well, hopefully the house is move-in ready and if it is, we're going straight to Wickes and buy some furniture. Don't cry Bay, everything will be alright!" Jason held Shameka in his arms as she wept.

$

KK and Dog Eye sat in the back of the narc car as it rode along the bank of the river.

"Yo, this ain't the way to the jail pig!" KK screamed to the officers from the back seat.

"Hey son, I'm about to cut you guys a break, so I don't think it's wise to disrespect us right now."

"What you talking about a break? Police don't give niggas breaks!"

"Why don't you just shut up KK? If they said they going to cut us a break, shit, I'M NOT TRYING TO GO TO JAIL!" Dog Eye pleaded to KK while crying like a little baby.

"You shut up bitch nigga. If they let us go, I'm a fuck you up anyway!"

While KK was talking shit to Dog Eye, the police officer screamed for both of them to shut up.

"Look, we need both of your parents' addresses and then yall are free to go."

Dog Eye shouted his mom's address out as soon as the words left the officer's mouth.

"Ok, now what about you KK?"

"2370 Federal Ave."

"Hey son, if you're telling me a lie, you will pay for it. Believe me, you will pay for it!" Josh assured KK.

As they let Loose out of the car, a guy from the car that was following walked up and shoved a knife through the back of Dog Eye's neck. KK screamed and cried as he watched Dog Eye's lifeless body fall to the ground.

"Please don't kill me! What did I do? I did nothing to you! Please sir, please!" KK pleaded as the man opened the back door and yanked him out the backseat.

KK screamed as one of the guys slammed him to the ground as the other guy started to cut his hand off. He screamed as if the pain was unbearable.

After cutting KK's hand off, he put the bloody hand in a zip lock bag before walking over to the lifeless body on the other side of the car. While KK laid on the ground, Josh shoved a knife through the back of his head, killing him instantly. Paul cut the hand off of Dog Eye's dead body and drugged the body into the river.

After bagging up Dog Eye's hand, he drugged KK's lifeless body into the river as well. Josh grabbed the bag with KK's hand in it and told Paul to take the other one to the address Dog Eye had given them. Both cars calmly pulled off.

$

As the night wound down, Jason made love to Shameka while his twin brother Jermaine was still sound asleep over Rashawnda's. Gold was taking care of his Larimer niggas before heading back to fuck the shit out of Yalonda. Spade was riding around on the North Side looking for KK and Dog Eye, wanting revenge, even after Jason told him that Gold was taking care of them niggas.

Chapter 10

The next morning, Jermaine woke up next to Mia and Rashawnda half-naked in the same bed as him. He smiled as he remembered what happened yesterday.

He reached for the remote and turned the TV on. As he flicked through the channels, he stopped as breaking news coverage flashed on Channel 11.

"Breaking news you will only see on Channel 11. Last night, Pittsburgh Police arrived at a call at 2370 Federal Avenue. The complaint was that someone had left a zip lock bag with a bloody human hand inside. It was left on the porch of Vicky Sims. Twenty minutes later, they were called to the residence of Tanny Rivers, where she also found a zip lock bag with a bloody human hand inside. This is Donna Summers, reporting the news. Hear more about this story tonight on News at 11."

Pittsburgh has never had a crime like this occur before and detectives were as puzzled as they have ever been. Tanny and Vicky were both nervous and worried because neither of them were able to get in touch with their sons.

"Hello!"

"Yo, you woke Bro?"

"Naw, not for real, what's up?" Jason said in a tired voice.

"Yo, I was just watching the news right, and they just found a bloody hand in a bag on this lady's porch! Yo Bro, there's some crazy mafuckas out here Ike!"

"Oh yeah, that's crazy! Yo, you still up shorty's crib?"

"Yeah!"

"Well, I left the work at Mom's house, so separate that shit for me Ike. After you're done, meet me at Shameka's crib so I can give you this dough to go grab you a phone."

"Aiight, I'm a go do that now. I'll be at Shameka's in like an hour."

"That's what's up, see you when you get here, One." Jason pressed the end button on his phone as he turned over to try to go back to sleep.

As Jermaine hung up Rashawnda's phone, he smacked Mia on her ass to wake her up.

"Yo, I'm out Bay, come lock the door," Jermaine said while putting his left leg into his jeans and pulling his pants up.

"Oh, you leaving Bay?" Mia asked as she wiped the crust out of the crevices of her eyes.

"Yeah, I have to handle some business, but I'm trying to see you later ma." He said as he reached down and rubbed her clit assuring her that he wanted to see her again later.

"See, you playing now. Here, come lie down and let me suck it before you leave."

She pulled him back onto the bed and instantly started to zip his pants down. She began sucking his dick, giving him fast wet strokes as she tried to make him cum quick.

"Damn, share that dick Bitch!" Rashawnda said after being woke up by the movement of the bed.

"Girl, I didn't know you were woke," Mia replied while briefly taking Jermaine's dick out of her throat. She reached her right arm behind her, trying to pull Rashawnda up closer to his dick. They both took turns deep throating and stroking him one after the other.

"Awwww yeah... I'm about to cum ma, don't stop!" Jermaine moaned as he shot an over-sized load down Mia's throat."

"Mmmm Bay, that was a lot," Mia said as she swallowed the large amount of semen.

"Damn Bitch, you could have saved me some!" Rashawnda stated as she began licking the slobber and remaining cum off Jermaine's dick.

$

"Hey Ms. Vicky, I just seen what happened on the news. I meant to call you last night. The police arrested KK at my house last night ---"

"Oh, Thank You Lord, Thank You! Asia, you don't know how worried I was. THANK YOU LORD! THANK YOU LORD! Asha, I'll call you back. Thanks for calling me and letting me know that my baby is ok!"

As soon as Vicky hung up the phone, she told the detectives that it was not the hand of her baby and that he was arrested last night on Pennsylvania Ave.

After receiving the news, the detectives called into headquarters to check on the arrest of Kevin Kelly and held on the line as they searched the database. They could not find a current arrest report for the name Kevin Kelly, only being able to find previous records, but none for yesterday's date.

"Excuse me, Ms. Vicky it is right?"

"Yes!"

"Um, I just had my Headquarters check on an arrest for your son and they were not able to retrieve one. Who told you he was arrested?"

"His girlfriend, she said they arrested him last night at her house," Vicky responded as her fear came back that it might be the hand of her son.

"Can you get Kevin's girlfriend on the phone for me Ms. Vicky? I have a few questions to ask her."

Vicky frantically called Asia's phone back.

"Hello!" Asia said as she answered her phone.

"Hi, this is Detective Shawn Green and I have a few questions to ask you."

"Ok!"

"Did you see the officers that arrested Kevin?"

"No, I didn't know he was being arrested. I happened to look out the window and saw two narc cars pulling off from in front of my house."

"Did you see Kevin inside of one of the cars?"

"Yes, and it looked like they had someone in the back with him."

"Ok, and your name?"

"Asha, Asha Parks."

"Ok Asha, I'll be keeping in touch."

The detectives started to smell foul play. Two narc cars that seemed like they were not the department's cars, two people in the back of only one of them, and two severed hands, at two different residences. Something was definitely not right.

$

"Who is it?" Ms. Bell screamed.

"Jermaine."

"Hi you doing Jermain," Ms. Bell said as she opened the door.

"I'm ok, is my brother woke?"

"I don't know. Sit here while I go and get him."

As Ms. Bell went to get Jason, Jermaine sat on the couch, wondering if she knew that the bag he held was full of drugs.

"Jermaine, he's in Shameka's room, go head back."

As Jermaine walked in the room and sat on the chair inside Shameka's room, Jason asked, "Yo, what's good Bro? Did you do that yet?"

"Yeah, it was ten bricks."

"Ten, I thought that bag felt heavier than usual. Well, shit, that's more dough for us. Since these shootings got the block hot, I'm a just see if the three main buyers want to double up this go round."

"That sounds like a plan. I'm a go see dude's sister today so I could get his number."

"Yeah do that because I know this nigga Booman that be moving that shit like crazy on the Westside."

Jason gave Jermaine some money to get a phone as he called the three main buyers. All three of them took his offer to double up.

He stood to profit a hundred and fifty thousand today off this package, so paying the lady a hundred stacks for the house would be nothing. After buying the house, he would still have fifty thousand, and that would be the fifty he would use to buy the heroin off of Jermaine's man. He decided that from this point on, he was not touching the money he had put away.

$

"Goldie, did you see the news my boy?"

"Naw, why, what's wrong?"

"Let's just say I *hand*-led it for you! Hahahahahaha! See you when you're ready to reup my boy. Hahahaha!"

Gold wasn't sure what Akbatu was talking about so he turned on the news. Not even five minutes of watching, he read a headline that said two bloody severed hands were found at two different locations.

Gold was shocked on how Josh handled KK and Dog Eye and figured he did it that way for one reason – to let him know not to ever try to fuck him. It was a scare tactic that Gold would take serious. Serious enough to hurry up and get Jason ready to take his place.

"Yo, where you at Bro?" Gold asked.

"About to make these moves before I have Shameka call that lady for the house."

"Ok well I'm ready when you are. Yo, how much did she say she wanted?"

"Like a hundred thousand. I was going to give her ninety cash and see if she will let go for that."

"And you were going to have the feds all over us. You can't spend that type of money in cash. I'm a give her a cashier's check so don't even worry about it. Consider it a present from me to you Bro."

"Word! That's what's up Ike! But, I got the money yo, especially since you gave me those extra joints. I could pay for the house with the profit off that alone Ike."

"Naw, you good. Besides, you need to stack your dough. You never know how long this type of life will last, so you got to hold on to what you got youngin', remember that!"

"You right Bro. Well, let me take care of this business and I'll call you when I'm done. One." Jason said before pressing the end button on his phone.

Everything was working out for Jason. He would be turning eighteen years old in eight months. He almost got half a million stashed and his brother was home to help him maintain and prosper. He thought to himself, "What a life!" The only thing that bothered him was his crew. He started feeling like they were holding him back. All the bullshit Spade got him in with them North Side niggas was fucking with him. Little Larry getting shot was weighing heavy on him and he was starting to blame himself. Lyrics by the great 2 Pac began playing in his head:

"I see no changes...wake up in the morning and I ask myself...is life worth living should I blast myself...I'm tired of being poor even worse I'm black...my stomach hurts so I'm looking for a purse to snatch...cops give a damn about a negro...pull a trigger kill a nigga he's a hero...give the crack to the kids who the hell cares...one less hungry mouth on the welfare...first ship em' dope and let em' deal to brothers...give em' guns step back and watch em' kill each other...It's time to fight back, that's what Huey said...two shots in the dark now Huey's dead...I got love for my brother... but we could never get nowhere unless we share with each other...We gotta start making changes...learn to see me as your brother instead of two distant strangers...and that's how it's supposed to be...how can a Devil take a brother if he's close to me... I'd love to go back to where we played as kids...but things change, that's just the way it is... That's just the way it is ~ things will never be the same ~ That's just the way it is ~ Awww yeah..."

Chapter 11

Six months have gone past and everything was going as planned. Jason fell back from the crew he was running with, leaving Spade and a few others broke and searching for ways to get paid.

After recovering, Lil Larry decided that the game wasn't for him, so he took some G.E.D classes, hoping to further his education afterwards. Mia ended up leaving Zoe and her and Rashawnda started to really fuck around, blessing Jermaine as he somewhat wifed the both of them.

Jason and Jermaine hooked up with the dope connect and were flooding Booman with bricks of stamp bags. Booman had the Westside on lock, controlling the whole Broadhead, Westgate and half of Chartiers. Booman was bringing the twins at least sixty thousand a week, plus Jason now had five buyers copping constantly every two weeks.

Gold wasn't aware of the twins being involved with the dope game and was planning to introduce Jason to Akbatu during the next flip. It was time for him to disappear to a nice house down in Florida. Gold felt bad knowing that he was setting the twins up for a lifetime of crime, but he was ready to be able to enjoy his success. He was sitting on like three million in drug money and two million in legit cash that had accumulated in his stock portfolio during a good year of trading.

$

"Yo, this nigga Jason got me hot for real! It's been like three months and this nigga still ain't get on. It's biting out this bitch! I'm mad as hell Ike!" Spade expressed his frustration to Rated as he watched him make like six sales.

"I told you already Ike, you better start going to see Butter. He be showing me love Ike," Rated replied as he wrapped the bag of crack up and put it inside the mail box.

It's been three months since Spade last paid Jason and Jason was yet to call him to reup. Spade never saved his money and was always waiting for Jason to front him or let him work the North Side trap.

"Shit, my money is funny right now. I only got like two stacks to play with Ike. What you think Butter will give me for that?" Spade asked Rated.

"Shit, like two zips. He be charging eleven, but I could get you two Ike. He be charging me a stack for a whole one. Want me to call him Ike?"

"Yea yup Ike, call that nigga. I can't keep missing this dough Ike." Spade stated as he cracked the blunt that he was about to roll up.

They sat in the hallway talking and smoking while waiting on Butter to call Rated's phone back. It would be Spade's first time buying his own work and he was a little unsure on how he would profit. He wouldn't be able to sale no weight and was going to have to sell it all to the fiends. That wasn't something he was used to. He was used to taxing niggas like fifty to a hundred dollars extra as they copped quarters and whole ones. That was how he got his dough, so not being able to serve the hustlers was a serious concern. He just hoped Jason would be getting on and back at him soon.

$

"Yo my dude, you know I got the best dope in Pittsburgh. You should get down with me homey," Booman stated to Thug as he sat on the porch of one of his trap houses in Chartiers.

"Oh yea, what's the prices like my dude? Because I'm getting my bags cheap as hell, but if you can beat two hundred a brick, we might be able to make it happen my dude." Thug responded to Booman's offer.

"The best I could do is one-seventy-five a brick. I usually charge two-twenty-five, but like I said, I got the best dope in the city." Booman gave Thug his number and told him to call when he's ready to make moves. Thug had the upper part of Chartiers on lock, moving at least a hundred bricks a day and half of them were to the fiends.

He was killing em! By pulling Thug in, Booman would now supply the whole Westside.

Booman was a true hustler, a fast talker and didn't hesitate to bust his guns. One day, he shot a nigga in the face for shorting him only seventy dollars for a package that cost three thousand. That's the type of nigga he was, quick to pull that Point 40 out. Straight Head Buster, a nigga that you didn't want to cross if you knew what was best for you.

After logging in Thug's phone number Booman walked back into the trap and called Jermaine. He was running low on bricks and needed to make sure he had a enough work for when Thug called.

"What's up my dude? I'm ready to reup, they loving that shit my dude! Plus, I got a new nigga from Chartiers that's going to be calling me soon."

"Yo, this shit going to be here for a while Ike! But, what's up with that new nigga you talking about Ike? You know there is a lot of snitch niggas out here!"

"Look my dude, I'm going out blazing if those boys ever come for me, that's my word! And this whole Westside know what it is if a mother fucker snitch on me!"

"Ha ah ah, I know that's right Ike. Well, I'm going to call you when I'm on my way." Jermain laughed at the statement Booman made as he pressed the end button on his phone.

$

"Girl, Gold got this bag of money that been here for at least three months. I wonder if he forgot about it," Linda said to Jen as they sat in her living room.

"Girl, you know as soon as you touch that bag Gold will be coming around looking for it. Besides, you don't need no extra money bitch, the way our girls is bringing that money in."

"You right, we don't need no bad karma," Linda replied as she passed Jen the blunt of purple haze.

After that surprising night with Gold, Linda and Jen decided to partner up and run an escort service. They recruited ten young strippers, five from Philly and five from Cleveland. They were all different sizes, colors and backgrounds, but they all had the same dream – to fuck their way out of the trap of poverty.

"Linda, did you see the Italian guy that requested Tamirra last night? Wooo girl, this mother fucker was fine girl, you hear me!" Jen stated to Linda as she inhaled the thick smoke through her nose that tried to escape form her mouth.

"Well, she better come correct this week because the bitch was short last week!" Linda replied while squirting lotion into her hand.

She put lotion on her legs as she sat on the couch, legs wide open, pussy looking like a peach. Jen couldn't help but to notice and the sight was turning her on. She watched as Linda's hands rose closer to her crouch. She envisioned that it was her hands rubbing Linda's legs. She tried to fight back the temptation as she began to get moist.

$

"Tu non rispondi piu al telefono ~ E aprendi filo ogni speranza mia ~ Io non avrei creduto mai di poter perder la testa per te ~ All improvise sei fugato via ~ Lasciando il vuoto in questa vita mia ~ Senza rispost ai miei perche adesso cosa mi resta di te ~ Non c'e' non c'e ilprofuma della pelle..."

As the Italian music by Laura Pausini played softly in the background, Antonio gently rubbed on Tamirra's ass, kissing and caressing her thighs. He was sprung and this was his third time requesting her this month. Taking her home with him wasn't possible, but the thought have crossed his mind a few times. Antonio was a member of an Italian Pittsburgh mob family which prohibit any members of being emotionally involved with any other race but their own. He was ready to get whacked about that young black pussy.

"Well baby, it's time for me to go. I had a really good time. I hope you did as well." Tamirra said as she rolled over to put her panties on.

"Oh darling, how about I give you two thousand more dollars for you to spend the day with me."

"Umm, I think I could make that happen, but you got to take me back to check in first. My dues are due every Monday morning."

"Ok, ok, well let's get you over there so we could finish relaxing because *mi piace stare con te*!" Antonio finished his statement in Italian, saying that he loved being with

$

Temptation ended up getting the best of Jen. She was now on all fours licking Linda's pussy as Linda's hand gripped the back of her head, guiding her to each side. Jen licked gently between Linda's pussy lips before spreading them open with her thumbs. She then began to insert her tongue inside of her. As Linda began to shake and moan, they were distracted by the doorbell. [Ding dong – Ding dong]

"WHO IS IT?"

"It's Tamirra!"

"Oh, hold up girl!" Jen yield as she stood up to go open the door.

"Hi you doing this morning Miss Jen?"

"I'm good. You're here kind of early girl."

"I know. My trick wanted to pay me double to stay another day with him and I didn't want to be late paying my dues, so I had the mother fucker bring me pass girl. So, here you go, this is thirteen hundred. Tell Miss Linda I said hi and I will see you ladies tomorrow."

"Well ok girl and bitch be safe!" Jen said to Tamirra before closing the door.

After closing the door, Jen turned around and she noticed Linda coming out of her room fully dressed.

"Well damn girl, wasn't it good?!"

"Yeah, of course girl, I just have some shit to handle. Why don't you call Gold for me and see if he wants to join us later? I would like that," Linda replied.

"Well Tamirra gave us thirteen hundred. Italian dude paid her double to spend an extra day with him. Shit, she got her claws in that nigga."

Without replying, Linda kissed Jen on the lips and walked out the door. Jen couldn't help but to feel like she was a trick because Linda ran off like one of the girls would have after getting paid.

$

"What's up Lil Bro, I got to talk to you, where you at?"

"I'm in the crib. What's up with you?"

"Nothing serious, I'm on my way to your crib be there soon."

"That's what's up. I'll see you when you get here," Jason replied to Gold before hanging up.

"Yo, Gold on his way Ike," he informed Jermain before grabbing the gun off the coffee table.

"Oh yeah! Gold been asking too many questions lately Bro. The nigga asked my why don't we be fucking with Spade?"

"He asked you that? Why the nigga just ain't ask me? Yeah, that's weird as hell! Here this nigga go now. That was fast as hell. He must have been right around the block or some shit when he called."

As Gold pulled into the driveway, Jason opened up the front door, waving his hand, motioning for Gold to just come in. Jason wasn't sure what Gold was coming to talk about and was a little bit frustrated about him asking Jermaine shit that he could have asked him. Jason had been getting these bad vibes from Gold lately, but he couldn't put his finger on why.

"What's up with my two little niggas?"

"Yo Gold, I ain't been little in a while now," Jermaine joked.

Jason replied by saying he was good. The tension in the room was thick as Gold sat on the couch. Jason proceeded to cracking the Swisher. Gold broke the eerie silence in the air.

"So look, I got to go out of town for a minute and Jason, (he clears his throat) I'm gonna need you to see Akbatu for me in my absence."

"Gold, dude don't even know me!"

"I told him about you already. I told him I had some business and that I was sending you in my place. All you have to do is meet him at the hotel, drop him the cash and he's going to hand you the duffel bag and that's that. Nigga, just like you used to do when you were younger," Gold replied before dropping a laundry bag on the floor.

He continued, "This is three hundred thousand, the two-fifty we owe and fifty for the reup. And Jason, when I get back, I'm gon' show you a way out of this shit. My flight leaves at four, so I need to be on my way. Dude is going to call you. Hit me and let me know everything is good." The words rushed out of his mouth as he stood up to leave.

As soon as he was out the door and in his whip, Jermaine said, "Yo that was some bullshit Bro! That shit don't sound right!"

"I know, but guess what? I ain't going to see nobody! Who the fuck do he think I am? I'm keeping this money Bro! I'm done selling that shit anyway. I'm a dope boy now!" Jason replied as he took a pull of the blunt of purple.

Oh, speaking of dope, I got to go meet Booman," Jermaine said as he grabbed his phone off the table.

"Damn! He ready already?" Jason asked.

"Yeah, he be doing the damn thing Bro. I'm out. I'll hit you later."

After Jermaine left Jason sat in his living room and pondered on what he was going to do about going to see

Akbatu. He didn't trust it and had a bad vibe about the whole thing.

He really didn't want to keep the three hundred thousand and was thinking of a way to give Akbatu the money without having to go himself. As he sat and thought, Spade came to mind. He hasn't talked to Spade in a few months, but figured Spade would be pressed to make some money. The proposition he would make to Spade will be undeniable.

Chapter 12

"What's up ma?" Gold said as he answered his phone.

"Hey baby, what are you doing," Jen asked in a seductive way.

"Chilling, on my way to the mall. What's up with you Bay?"

"Well you know you left this bag of money over here right?"

"Oh shit, yeah, I almost forgot about that bag! It's been a lot of shit on my mind. Sheesh!"

"Well come let me and Linda relieve some of that stress!"

"That sounds like a plan! I'll be through in a minute ma."

"Ok, I'll see you when you get here."

"That's what's up. One."

Gold pressed the end button on his phone. He felt bad knowing he was setting Jason up and decided that getting pleased by two beautiful women would help clear his conscience. He had left that money for Linda and Jen, thinking he would never see them again, which was his plan, but he figured while he had a few hours before his plane took off, why not have a little fun before he go.

$

"Yo, who's this?" Spade said as he answered his phone.

"Jason!"

"Damn nigga, I thought you ain't fuck with me. I ain't heard from you in months!"

"I know yo, I had to fall back for a while, but I need to rap to you in person. I might have a love shot for you."

"Oh yeah! I need it Ike. It been ugly out here."

"Well you might be able to change that. Yo, meet me in my mom's old court. I'll be there in like forty minutes."

"That's what's up, I'll be there. One."

Spade was a new person after that call. The pain of being broke was turned into ambition and the next forty minutes felt like the longest forty minutes of his life. He had to smoke at least three blunts of fifty. Each minute felt like an hour and his patience was running thin. Finally, Spade saw Jason pulling up in an older model caravan.

"What's up Ike," Jason said as he hopped out the van.

"What's good Stranger, what's up with this fucking caravan nigga," Spade replied with a chuckle in his voice.

"Yo, the pigs don't even look at shit like this. I'm low-key in this bitch. Anyway Ike, I got a love shot for you."

"Ok, what we talking?"

"Look, Gold had to go out of town today, but he wanted me to reup for him while he was gone. But for real Spade, I'm done with all this shit yo, so I don't really want to make the move, feel me?"

"Yeah, but what do all this got to do with me?"

"I was thinking earlier about how you took care of that business when I was in Jamaica. That was some real shit Ike and I never told you how much I appreciated that Ike. So, I was thinking that I'll I let you go meet the connect and put you on Ike. Shit, you can even have my phone. There's five niggas that call this phone twice a month for two keys a piece."

"Word! Do you think Gold would be cool with that?"

"Yeah, but even if he wasn't, fuck him! Nigga you killed niggas before!"

"Aiight then, fuck him! When is all this going to happen?"

"Sometime tomorrow Akbatu will call this phone."

"Akbatu?"

"Yeah, that's the connects name Ike. Look, this is all you got to do. I'm going to give you three hundred thousand. Two-fifty is what we owe him and the other fifty is for the reup. Go meet him, give him the money and he's going to give you ten keys. When you're done, take him three hundred thousand and yall gon' do it again. It's that simple!"

"Shit, fuck that, I'm with it Ike! I'm tired of being broke!"

"Aiight then, here go my phone and here go the money," Jason said as he reached in the caravan to grab the bag.

"Yo, good looking my nigga! You know you one crazy mother fucker driving around with three hundred thousand on you," Spade said as Jason got back in the van.

$

"Damn girls, I'm a miss fucking with yall," Gold said to Linda and Jen as he tried to catch his breath. The three had just finished the best threesome he had in his life.

"Why you say that? Why would you miss us?" Linda asked.

"I got to go to Philly later. I'm thinking about staying. That's why I left that dough here. That was for yall. It was like a goodbye gift."

"Oh, you was just going to blaze like that my nig," Jen said as she pulled up her panties.

"Naw, it wasn't like that, I was going to call and let yall know I was good."

"So what made you decide to want to move to Philly," Linda asked.

"My peoples is up there and I'm just ready for a change. Bay, I have a lot of demons in this city that I need to escape from, so I'm a use this opportunity to get out while I can," Gold replied as he lit the half of blunt that was in the ashtray.

Gold told the girls to buy themselves something nice with the money. They sat and smoked while reminiscing about the first time they all kicked it that night Gold got back from Jamaica. After finishing the blunt, he left.

He called Yolanda and told her, that she could be on her way to the airport. He was ready and had everything mapped out to the tee. He would finally be able to enjoy life.

$

"Hello, Is this Jason?" A Turkish voice said as Spade answered the phone Jason gave him.

"Naw, Jason ain't around right now. He wanted me to take care of this. Is this Akbatu?"

"That depends. Are you a cop?"

"Naw I ain't no mutha-fucking cop! I'm Jason's man, Spade."

"Oh ok, well you need to be at the Omni Hotel at nine o'clock. Suite 1650. Bring the money with you."

"I'll be there."

As Spade pressed the end button on his phone, he contemplated on if he wanted to go through with it. He wanted to just keep the money. Three hundred g's could put him right where he wanted to be, but he was a loyal soldier and crossing Jason wasn't something he wanted to do.

$

"Ok Booman, you got it banging out this mafucka," Jermaine said as he passed Booman the blunt.

"This is what I do my dude. Fuck and get money! I got these shorties on their way now to gun us down my dude! This is how it goes down on this side."

While talking to Booman, Jermaine got a call from Jason.

"What's up Bro?"

"Shit, sitting here with Booman, waiting on these hoes to come through. What's up with you?"

"About to go pick up Shameka, but yo, we might have problems when Gold get back."

"Why you say that?"

"Yo, I gave Spade that money to go see Akbatu."

"Oh yeah, why you do that?"

"Something just didn't feel right Bro."

"I know, I was feeling the same thing! Well fuck it, I'll do Gold if I have to Bro..."

"What, yall need somebody to disappear my dude," Booman said when he heard Jermaine statement about murder.

"Yo, Booman just asked if we needed someone to disappear."

"Oh yeah, tell that nigga I said what's up. But yeah, I was just calling to let you know what I did. I'm a call Spade tomorrow to see what happened."

"Aiight, I'm about to let this bad ass shorty gun me down Bro, I'll hit you later or in the morning."

"Aiight then. One."

Jermain grabbed the shorty as he pressed the end button on his phone.

$

"Excuse me, what elevators go to the 16th floor," Spade asked the lady at the front desk.

"The middle bank to your left," the lady replied.

As Spade walked to the elevators, his heart trembled. He wanted to turn around and leave, but figured he came this far and this could be the deal of his lifetime. He proceeds onto the elevator as two foreigners got on with him. As the elevator began to ascend, Spade was startled by the feeling of cold steel on the back of his head.

"Here, the money is in the bag! Please don't kill me!" Spade pleaded.

"Shut your nigger mouth," the foreigners said as he shoved Spade off of the elevator once they reached the 16th floor.

"What did I do?" Spade cried as he was being pushed and shoved down the hall.

"You niggers think shit don't stink!"

As they reached the suite, they shoved him through the doors.

"Josh, Josh, why so rough? Stand up boy. So Spade it is, right?" While rubbing his chin with his thumb and his pointing finger Akbatu asked Spade his name as if he didn't know it.

"Yeah! I'm the one you talked to on the phone. I thought everything was cool, what did I do," Spade asked Akbatu as he stood to his feet.

"Oh nothing, Josh just has a problem with black people. Did you bring the cash?"

"Yeah, its three hundred g's in the bag. Fifty of which is mine. I was hoping we could do business. Jason said he was done with the game. That's why he sent me."

"Is that right? So Jason thinks he can just stop when he feel like it? Well I got something for people like him. Spade, so you want to do business huh? Well, here's what I'm going to do for you. I'm going to give you twenty kilos and you will bring me back four hundred thousand. Can you handle that boy?"

"Hell yeah!"

"Ok and I will need that by this time next month."

"Shit, I could do that!"

"But there is two catches. If I give you my product, there will be no quitting! Do you understand me? And I want to read about Jason's death in Monday's paper."

Spade agreed as Akbatu handed him the duffel bag of coke. He was happy to be living, but had a hard weekend in front of him. He didn't think he could do it. Him and Jason had been close friends since they were kids. "It's going to be hard, but it got to be done," Spade thought to himself.

$

"It would be so nice (nice, nice) If you didn't have to feel so lonely... It would be so nice (nice, nice) If I could sneak you for a moment...I know you like to get away, go away, far away...To a place where it's just us two....Got a busy day, every day, but not today...Cause I'm here to take that stress from you...So you could just chill and clear your head...And let me do everything for you cause you deserve it...Prepare your meal and make your bed...Willing to switch places with you cause you are so worth it."

Then Akon added his melody, "I just want us to go-go-go-go...Drop everything and just go-go-go...I just want us to go-go-go-go...Drop everything and just go go go go... How would like to sail away in the Bahamas...Just you and me girl...So far out in the sea where nobody could find you...Just the end of the world...Cause there is no rush to come back to the rain...Cause there is plenty sunshine where I'm picking you...And I'm here to reduce the pain...I know you like to get away, go away, far away...To a place where just us two..."

As the words from the song "Just Go" by Lionel Richie and Akon massaged Shameka's brain, Jason's tongue massaged between her thighs. While barely able to talk, she told Jason to give her a baby and as the words left her mouth, tears rolled down her face. She was in love and was ready to give Jason a reason to leave all this shit alone. Jason picked his head up and began to make hard, passionate love to her.

His mind was also made up and all he wanted was to be able to live a happy life. The thought of being able to live that life with Shameka would be a dream come true and he was in a position to make it all happen.

Chapter 13

Jason woke up to the sun shining through the window, and was admiring the way the sun beamed up against Shameka's face. While lying there, Jason thought long and hard about the move he made yesterday. He was second guessing himself. "Was it really a good move to give that money to Spade," he thought. "Would Spade run off with the money?" It was all starting to bother him, so he got up and called Spade to see what it was hitting for.

"Yo, who this?" Spade answered in a tired voice.

"Jason Ike, did you handle that?"

"Oh yeah, good looking Ike, this move going to change my life! We should get out tonight Ike. Go pop a few bottles, my treat for once!"

"Oh yeah, that's what's up, we could do that. I haven't been out in a while, but yo, I'm a hit you later Ike. One."

After talking to Spade, Jason felt a lot better. He wanted to call Gold, but decided not to. Mainly due to the fact that he still had a funny feeling about the way Gold just left.

"Hey baby, you're up early. What are you doing," Shameka asked as she walked into the living room.

"Just got off the phone with Spade."

"Spade? I haven't heard that name in a while."

"I know. I needed him to do something for me yesterday."

"Oh, did everything work out?"

"Yeah yup, but Shameka, what you think about selling the house and moving out of town?"

"I wouldn't mind moving, but where to?"

"I was thinking ATL. Me, you and that baby we made last night," Jason said as he wrapped his arms around her.

"I don't know Jason. What about your brother, you just going to leave him here?"

"Naw, he could come if he wants to. Shit, he might want to stay here, but me, I'm ready to get the fuck out of here Bay! I never told you this, but for the last couple months, shit out in them streets have been weird. Gold been acting weird, this nigga Booman my brother's cool with seem too real to be real!"

"Well Baby, you got to go off of what your gut tell you and if you want to leave, shit, I'm with you!"

"I know Baby, that's why I love you," Jason replied as he kissed her.

His mind was made up, but talking Jermaine into leaving would be another story. A story he prayed

Jermaine will give in to. Jason figured he would go at him on some music shit being that Jermaine developed a nice rap game while he was locked up. That would really be his only hope to getting him to go.

$

"Yo my dude, your phone keeps ringing."

"Oh shit, where all these hoes come from Ike?"

"You was high as hell my dude. You slept through all that shit yo! They were eating each other, shit, I fucked four out of the six of them," Booman said to Jermain as he woke up.

"Yo, what's up Bro," Jermaine said after answering his phone.

"Yo, I need to talk to you Bro. Where you at?"

"On the Westside."

"Oh, well meet me at my crib in like twenty minutes."

"Aiight, I'll be there Ike." Jermaine pressed the end button on his phone as Booman passed him the blunt. They smoked while Booman told him about all the fun he missed last night.

After finishing the blunt, he told Jermaine he needed to reup. Booman made like forty thousand yesterday while fucking and having fun. "This is the life," Jermaine thought to himself.

"Aiight, I got you. I'll be back at like four, but you got to put it in the bags yourself this time Ike."

"That's what's up, I could do that my dude."

"Aiight then, I'm out Ike, hit you later." Jermaine dapped Booman up before he left.

As Jermaine got into his 5.0, he turned up his music before pulling off. He didn't know what Jason wanted to talk about, but he hoped that it wasn't about Spade running off with Akbatu's money. Jermaine really didn't think giving Spade that money was a good idea. He wanted to keep it and just say fuck Gold and Akbatu.

$

"Where you going Bay," Shameka asked as Jason walked out to the hallway by their bedroom.

"Nowhere, downstairs to wait on Jermaine."

"Oh okay, do you want me to get up and make yall some breakfast?"

"Naw I'm good Bay, thanks anyway," Jason replied as he walked down the steps. He was excited to put his own exit plan together and was hoping his twin would be a part of that plan.

He sat on his leather couch and rolled a blunt of purp while he waited. Five minutes into the blunt, Jermaine walked through the door.

"What's up with you Ike?"

"Ooohh, stressing Bro," Jason replied as he inhaled the thick smoke.

"I know shit been crazy these last couple days, but fuck it Bro, we did what we did and if Gold don't like it, that's on him. If he get hot, shit, I'll fill him up with something hotter. Did you call Spade yet to see if he made the move?"

"Yeah, he said everything went perfect. He wants to treat us to the club tonight."

"Oh yeah, that's what's up. He must be geeked up, he about to be on top," Jermaine replied as Jason passed him the blunt .They sat and smoked as they made small talk.

"So Bro, what did you want to talk about," Jermaine asked as he walked back into the living room with a glass of water.

"Yo, we got well over two million dollars Ike and this game is starting to get real dangerous. I'm thinking about quitting Bro. I want a better life than this."

"I feel you, but I thought that's why we switched to dope!"

"I switched to dope because it was more money. A faster way to get our money up, but we good now Bro."

"Aiight, what we going to do if we stop Bro, sell houses or some shit? We ain't even old enough to do anything else."

"I was thinking we get serious with the rap thing!"

"Bro, you know how hard it is to make it in the rap game in the Burgh?"

"Yeah, that's why I was thinking we go to ATL and try there."

"Just pick up and leave, huh Bro? What about mom? What, we going to leave her?"

"Naw nigga, she's coming with us! Look, we got money Bro. We could make it happen down there Ike, I'm telling you!"

"Jason, you my twin Ike and I can't see me here by myself so I'm in if you think we can make it happen. I'm with you nigga, I love you! So how much dope we got left, cause Booman ready to reup."

"It's like two keys left."

"Well when you plan on making this move?"

"In like two weeks, but I wanted to go down there tomorrow. Just to look around, check out a few things."

"That sound like a plan. Well, what do we want for those two keys?"

"Shit, how about sixty-five a piece?"

"He might not want both of them though."

"Tell him it's the last two and we can give them to him for a hundred and twenty thousand. He gone jump on it."

"Aiight, I'll hit you later," Jermaine said as he walked toward the door.

Jermaine wasn't really sold on this whole moving thing. He didn't mind stopping, but moving was a bit too much. He wasn't ready to leave all the fun behind. Besides, Jason had a two and a half year head start over him. He thought to himself, "Am I even that good with the rapping shit?"

Chapter 14

Jason, Jermaine and Booman arrive at Club 814 ready to relax, pop a few bottles and have a good night.

Jason was really celebrating his success and his departure from the game. Jermaine brought Booman just in case somebody started cutting up, knowing he didn't mind busting a nigga's head.

As they walked up to the VIP entrance, Spade was standing there waiting.

"Here go my niggas," Spade said as Jason and Jermain walked up.

"What's up Ike," Jason greeted upon walking up to him.

"I'm good now, feel me Ike!"

"Yeah, that's what's up, let's get in here and pop some bottles my nigga."

As they walked in, Spade never noticed that Booman was with them. Booman walked to a section of the club where he was able to see Jason and Jermain without anyone knowing he was watching.

"So what's good Jermaine, you still be fucking Mia?"

"Every once in a while, you know how it is."

"Yeah, they say she got bomb, I was trying…" Spade was interrupted by a bar maid telling him he was wanted in the bathroom. He got up to see who was checking for him.

"Yo, is it me, or this nigga Spade acting weird," Jermaine asked Jason as he swigged his bottle.

Meanwhile in the bathroom…

"Yo, you see what the nigga got on right?"

"Yeah."

"When he comes in this bathroom, I don't want to see him come out! You got that nigga!"

"I said yeah nigga, damn!"

"Aiight, well I'm a go back out there and finish kicking it. Yo, Ruger, don't fuck this up!"

"I'm not nigga, I got this!"

Spade walked out of the bathroom and back to the booth, "Aye Jason, roll that shit up Ikeee!"

"I'm rolling this shit now."

"Oh Bro, the real jakes be in this bitch. You better go roll that shit in the bathroom."

"Damn, it's like that in this bitch?"

"Hell yeah!"

"Aiight, I'll be back," Jason said as he got up to go roll the blunt in the bathroom. He had to piss anyway.

As Jason started walking towards the bathroom, Booman started towards it as well, taking a seat at a table nearest to it. Jason went inside and entered the first stall. He finished rolling his blunt, put it behind his ear and took a piss. As he walked out the stall, the bathroom attendant asked him if he needed a paper towel or some mouthwash. Being that he was about to smoke, he thought it would be a good idea to gargle some, so he walked over to the attendant. As he reached for the mouthwash, he felt a sharp pain in his stomach after hearing a bang.

Booman busted into the bathroom. The attendant then shot at Booman, missing him. Booman returned fire, hitting the attendant twice in the chest. After hearing the shots, Jermaine rushed to the bathroom area to find Booman dragging his brother out.

"Yo, that nigga Spade set us up," Booman said as Jermain made it over to them.

"Somebody call 9-1-1!!!!" Jermaine yelled as the people in the club started to scatter.

Booman and Jermaine managed to get Jason out the side door. The paramedics were in sight as Jermaine tried to keep his brother awake while crying and sobbing for revenge. Booman grabbed Jermaine's gun and keys and told him he would meet them at the hospital. As the paramedics put Jason inside of the ambulance, Jermaine heard them say that he should make it. Hearing them words lifted a ton of worries off of Jermaine.

$

After hearing all the shots, Spade ran with the crowd out of the club and got inside of his whip. He couldn't believe what he just made happen. His hands trembled as he turned the key to start the car before speeding off. He drove past the ambulance as the paramedics wheeled Jason into the back. He saw Jermaine look right at him as he sped pass. He knew it was going to be on. "It is what it is, Fuck em!" he said out loud to himself, keeping one eye on the road and one in the rearview mirror. He had twenty keys at the crib and always kept a boat load of guns. So with his money right and his guns right, he figured he was ready for a war.

See, Spade wasn't really a hustler. That's why Jason used to only let him run the North Side spot. He wasn't the go out there and get it type of nigga, but he was a true head buster and that's why Jason trusted him to work the spot. He knew Spade wouldn't be over there taking no bullshit and would crack a niggas head if they ever tried to pull some bullshit on him.

Spade figured he'd try and reach out to Jermaine in a few days so they wouldn't think he had something to do with the club shooting, but the look on Jermaine's face as he sped past told him that Jermaine already knew he was in on the shit, which meant he would definitely be retaliating. Spade didn't want to go to war for real, but he knew Jermaine wasn't going to let him get away with getting his twin killed and he definitely wouldn't be trying to hear no shit about Akbatu made him do it.

While pulling up to his house, he grabbed his nickel plated four-five from under his seat and cocked it. He was nervous and his hands trembled as he got out the car with the gun in his hand. He took quick steps through the gravel of his neighbor's driveway while constantly looking over his shoulders. He fumbled with his keys as he searched for his front door key. He worried that Jermain had already put a word out to some of their little goons to crack his head on sight if they see him.

After entering his apartment, he flopped down on the couch, relieved to be safe inside of his home. A lot has happened in the last thirty-six hours and he was yet to put it all together. He went from barely having flip fee, to having twenty keys that he needed to knock in twenty eight days or he'd also be going to war with Akbatu. He wondered how he was going to sell the keys while beefing with Jermaine.

As he started to roll a blunt, he was startled by the sound of his cell phone ringing.

"Yo Ike, where you at, it's biting out this bitch Ike," Rated asked Spade as soon as he answered the phone.

"I'm at the crib, but yo, I need to rap to you Ike. I can't talk over this phone though. Where can I meet you at Ike?"

"I'm up RC and I'm not moving. I told you it was biting out this bitch Ike," Rated said as he held the phone with his ear while counting about nine hundred dollars, most of it in fives and twenties.

"Yo, I'm going to make it worth your while Ike. Meet me at the Get-Go on Baum Boulevard in ten minutes," Spade replied as he pressed the end button on his phone.

Spade quickly changed out of the flashy clothes into some black dickies, black chucks, and a black hoody and was on his way.

$

"ONE, TWO, THREE, BREATHE! ONE, TWO, THREE, BREATHE! IT'S NOT LOOKING LIKE HE'S GOING TO MAKE IT! SET UP THE DEFIBRILATOR! COME ON SON, BREATHE! ONE, TWO, THREE, BREATHE! GOTDAMMIT, BREATHE!"

As Dr. Kenneth Moore performed CPR on the second gunshot patient of his twenty four hour shift, he was worried that he was going to lose this one. The bullet struck the bottom part of his heart and almost instantly sent him into cardiac arrest. Dr. Moore thought he felt a slight pulse and was franticly trying to save his second young black gunshot victim of the day.

The ER was packed and Dr. Moore was jumping around the hospital like crazy. After trying to shock the gunshot victim only once, because his Blackberry page alert sounded, he pronounced the guy dead. He rushed out of the room and back into the room where the first gunshot victim was being seen

He was in Room 3, in stable condition a minute ago, but was now starting to have complications with his kidneys. Doctor Moore ordered for a renal scan and told the nurse to get in touch with the phlebotomist to check his blood type. While the doctor's staff did what they were told, Dr. Moore went to the waiting room to inform the parents of the gunshot victim that died that they no longer had a son. After fifteen years of being a doctor, the conversation never got any easier.

"Is the family of Rudolph Thomas here," Dr. Moore asked as he walked into the waiting room.

"Yes! Please tell me my baby will be alright," Diane asked as she stood up and walked toward the doctor.

"You are Diane Thomas, the mother of Rudolph Thomas," he asked as he read her name off of Rudolph's hospital chart.

"Yes! How is my son doing," she asked with a more aggravated tone in her voice this time.

"I'm sorry I have to tell you this Ms. Thomas, but your son died at 2:47 am. We did everything we could have done to try and save him."

As he was breaking the bad news to Diane, she broke down in tears, sobbing and asking God to give her her baby back. The lady and her son that were sitting across from Diane watched as Diane dreadfully took in the bad news. They hoped that they weren't about to receive news of the same fate for their loved one who was being prepped for surgery.

After walking Diane to the family counsel department, Dr. Moore returned back to the ER's waiting room.

"How are you guys holding up over here," he asked Roxy and Jermaine as he walked over to them.

"We're doing good Doctor. How is Jason coming along," Roxy asked while unconsciously, tightly squeezing Jermaine's hand.

"Under the circumstances, he's doing well, but there is one potential problem. His kidneys are showing signs of failure. We're going to run a few more tests to be sure, but just in case, would you happen to know his blood type?"

"O negative," Roxy quickly answered.

"Did you say O negative," Dr. Moore asked as Roxy's answer took him by surprise.

"Yes, he's O negative and his twin here is O positive. I know it's rare. I was just as surprised when I found out."

"What you mean I'm positive Mom," Jermaine asked as if she was saying he was positive for some type of disease.

"Boy, I'm talking about yall blood type, now be quiet and let me talk to the doctor!"

"Well, yes, it's pretty rare for twins to have different blood types, but that's not what surprised me. What surprised me is how lucky your son may be right now. God must truly be with him!"

"LUCKY!" Roxy said as she slightly raised her voice.

"I meant no disrespect ma'am. I said he may be lucky because if his kidneys are failing, I have a young guy around his age that just passed away that's' O negative as well and would most likely be able to save your son's life," Dr. Kenneth Moore explained.

As he finished explaining Jason's situation to Roxy, Jermaine's mind wandered back to the club. He couldn't believe that they fell for Spade's trap. The sight of the two detectives entering the ER brought his thoughts back to the situation at hand as he told Roxy that he had to make a run and would be back later. He snuck out of the ER before the detectives were able to see him. He didn't feel like dealing with all the questions the D's would have lined up for him.

$

"Yo my dude, I need you to do me a big favor," Booman said to one of his boys as he walked into one of his traps on the Westside.

"What's that dude? I got a shorty coming through in a few my dude," his boy replied while barely taking his eyes off the sixty inch screen because he was getting his ass beat in Call of Duty.

Booman was already aggravated and at that time it didn't take much for him to snap. "WHAT THE FUCK MY DUDE!!! I SAID I NEED YOU TO DO ME A FAVOR YO!!! And you sitting here talking about some pussy yo!"

"OH SHIT!!! What the fuck happen my dude," his boy responded as he turned and saw all the blood that was smeared all over Booman's polo shirt.

"I was fucking with my Hill nigga at Club 814 and one of his own niggas tried to set his brother up! Yo, them Hill niggas is suckers my dude! My dude Jermaine real though and if that nigga's brother died, Shit!!! I know that nigga gone be putting in that work. But yo, I need you to go dump this burner for me while I change out of this shit," Booman said as he handed his boy the gun.

"Oh ok, yeah, I'll take care of that for you my dude, but shit got crazy up in that bitch huh," his boy asked as he wiped the burner off with his shirt.

"Hell yeah my dude, but the crazy shit is, I had the feeling some shit was going to pop off. This nigga Spade was acting weird as hell my dude. I don't see how Jason didn't see it yo, that shit was crazy. Yo! Any good in this bitch? I need to clear my head."

"Yeah, there's some pods of sour on the kitchen table," Booman's boy replied as he headed towards the door.

"YOOO, Why the fuck you got these bags all out like this," Booman screamed into the living room from inside the kitchen, but his boy was already out. He sat and finished bagging up the little bit of raw that his boy must have been bagging up before he got there.

$

As Jermaine walked out the side door of the hospital, he remembered that he left Jason's whip at the club and that Booman grabbed his burner while he was waiting for the ambulance to show up. "Shit," he said to himself, figuring he wouldn't make it too far trying to walk to the hood with all of his brother's blood on him. Good thing there was a jitney station close to the hospital, so he jogged to the station trying to stay out of sight of the cars that drove down Forbes Avenue.

Once he got to the station, he noticed that dick head Ron's car was the only car in front of the joint.

"Shit, I got to deal with this nigga, FUCK!" Jermaine said to himself as he knocked on the jitney station door.

"Where you want to go yougin'," Jitney Ron said in that fucked up ass voice of his.

"Warring Ct." Jermaine replied while trying to keep Ron from seeing all the blood that was on the front of his shirt. He knew if Jitney Ron seen all the blood, he wouldn't ride him and would probably call the police. Dude was an asshole like that.

Warring Court was only like five minutes away from the station, but it always seemed like a twenty minute ride when you rode with Ron. Eight minutes later, Jermaine was relieved to pull up in front of his old court. He paid Jitney Ron and got out of the car and headed towards Rashawnda's hallway.

He changed his clothes, grabbed his keys to his whip and the .38 special from up under the kitchen cabinet. He knew from the first day he came home that he was going to eventually have to crack Spade's head and tonight was the night. He promised himself that he wasn't going to let Spade live to see the sun rise.

He made a few phone calls trying to find out where Spade been staying but none of the people he called knew. He decided to ride up R.C. and ask the little bitch Spade was living with when the North Side niggas shot up her court. He dialed Shameka's number as he pulled off, realizing he never called and told her what happened to Jason.

"Hello," Shameka answered after like the fourth ring, clearly sounding like she was knocked out.

"Shameka!"

"Yeah, what's wrong? Where is your brother," she asked instantly, noticing it was like four in the morning.

"Jason got shot!"

"WHAT! IS HE OK? OH MY GOD! WHERE YOU AT?"

"Calm down Sis, the doctor said he should pull through! You know my brother's a soldier! But I just called to let you know he's at Mercy. I'll see you there in a little bit."

"Ok, well I'm on my way to the hospital. Be safe Bro," Shameka said before ending the call.

Jermaine put the burner in his hoody pocket as he got out the car and walked through the court. After going into the hallway, he quickly pulled it out after bumping into a fiend that stood in front of the steps - some wanna be tough, old stick-up man that was trying to get his chumpy lit. Jermaine thought he was going to have something slick to say, but he just continued trying to lite his pipe.

Jermaine put the burner back in his pocket and softly knocked on Spade's old bitch's door.

"Who is it," she asked.

"Jermaine! Sorry if I woke you up but it's important Bay," he said from the other side of the door.

"Hold up Jermaine," she responded as she got up off the couch that was next to the front door. "Hey, how have you been," she asked as she opened the door.

"Good Ma, I've been good and you," he replied, noticing how sexy shorty was.

"I been good, just been trying to survive, that's all."

"I know that's right Ma. Hey, have you seen Spade?"

"Not today, but he be hustling across the court. You know we don't' fuck around no more."

"Naw, I didn't know that. What happen?"

"Sheesh! It's a long story. More like what didn't happen."

"Oh okay, maybe you can tell me about it one day."

"Maybe!" she said, noticing the way he was looking at her.

"But yo, do you know where he's staying at?"

"Not really, but I know it's out East Liberty somewhere," she replied as she started to wonder why he was at her house at four in the morning.

"No disrespect ma, but do you let him still come through from time to time," he asked for two different reasons.

"If you're asking if we're still fucking, the answer is no! I can't stand that nigga no more!"

"Oh ok, well if you do see him, don't tell him I'm looking for him, ok pretty," he said while reaching for the door knob with his right hand and rubbing shorty's side with his left.

As he got back in the car, he called to see if Shameka made it to the hospital yet.

"Hello!"

"Did you make it to the hospital yet Sis?"

"Yeah, I'm here."

"Oh, ok, where is my mom at?"

"She's talking to the detectives."

"Oh, them fucks are still there huh?"

"Yeah, what happen Jermaine," she asked.

"I'll tell you later Sis, but keep me posted. I got to handle some shit right quick."

"Ok, be safe Bro! See you when you get here."

"Ok, one."

Jermaine pulled off and was on his way out East Liberty, determined to catch the nigga Spade. He couldn't believe what was going on, but knew exactly what he was going to do to this nigga when he caught him.

As he made the right down on Bigelow Blvd, he noticed the police at the other light. He drove with one eye in the mirror, hoping the police would make a right instead of following behind him. Seconds seemed like minutes and yards felt like miles before he was relieved, noticing that they made the right.

$

"So, you going to front a nigga a key and you only want twenty five back! Is that what you saying Ike," Rated asked as he leaned into the passenger side window.

"YEA NIGGA! Ain't that what I said Ike? We about to take over my nigga. I'll hit you as soon as I wake up Ike, ONE," Spade shouted out of his car window as he began to pull out the parking lot of the Get-Go.

He looked both ways, checking to make sure it was clear to pull out. He saw the head lights of a car coming toward him from the left, but notices it was about a mile away so he pulled out and made the right, speeding up to make it through the yellow light, only to catch the red at the next one. As his light changed green, so did the light behind him.

$

Jermaine notices a red Nova that was a few cars in front of him. It looked like Spade's whip, but he wasn't sure so he sped up to get a closer look. As he got a little closer, he noticed that it was indeed the nigga Spade. He slowed down and fell back as he followed him. He grabbed the .38 out of his hoody pocket and was about to speed up on the side of Spade and start banging, but the thought of the three hundred thousand dollars Jason gave him changed his mind. He figured it would be smarter to run up on Spade once he made it home. That way he could kill two birds with one stone – Murk Spade *and* get their dough back.

TO BE CONTINUED...

Made in the USA
Middletown, DE
06 February 2015